Dedalus Europe
General Editor: Timothy L

HUMAN SADNESS

GODERDZI CHOKHELI

HUMAN
SADNESS

edited by
Lia Chokoshvili

translated by
Geoffrey Gosby, Clifford Marcus,
Ollie Matthews, Margarert Miller
& Walker Thompson

Dedalus

This book is published with the support of the Writers' House of Georgia and Arts Council England.

Supported using public funding by
**ARTS COUNCIL
ENGLAND**

WRITERS'
HOUSE
OF GEORGIA

Published in the UK by Dedalus Limited
24-26, St Judith's Lane, Sawtry, Cambs, PE28 5XE
info@dedalusbooks.com
www.dedalusbooks.com

ISBN printed book 978 1 915568 50 2
ISBN ebook 978 1 915568 56 4

Dedalus is distributed in the USA & Canada by SCB Distributors
15608 South New Century Drive, Gardena, CA 90248
info@scbdistributors.com www.scbdistributors.com

Dedalus is distributed in Australia by Peribo Pty Ltd
58, Beaumont Road, Mount Kuring-gai, N.S.W. 2080
info@peribo.com.au www.peribo.com.au

First published by Dedalus in 2024
Printed and bound in the UK by Clays Elcograf S.p.A.
Typeset by Marie Lane

THE AUTHOR

GODERDZI CHOKHELI

Goderdzi Chokheli was born in 1954 in a small village north-east of Tbilisi, and died in Tbilisi in 2007. He was one of the most important filmmakers and prose writers of his era. He published one novel, *Human Sadness*, as well as a collection of short stories and some poetry. His films and screenplays won many awards both inside Georgia and abroad. In 1982 he was awarded the Grand Prize at the International Short Film Festival Oberhausen for his film *Easter*.

His unique place in Georgian society and culture is encapsulated by Levan Berdzenishvili: "Goderdzi Chokheli did not write anti-Soviet literature, he wrote non-Soviet literature. This is something that nobody else was able to do."

THE EDITOR
LIA CHOKOSHVILI

Lia Chokoshvili has been teaching Georgian at the University of Oxford for twenty-seven years. The Georgian Department at Oxford is funded by the Marjory Wardrop Fund which was set up in the early 20th century by the British diplomat Sir Oliver Wardrop to promote the study and teaching of Georgian. Both Oliver and his sister Marjory were translators so setting up a translation project in 2015 with her more advanced students seemed particularly appropriate to Lia. Various classic texts were translated and in 2021 the first ever English translation of one of the masterpieces of 20th-century Georgian literature, *Human Sadness*, by Goderdzi Chokheli was completed. The novel is narrated by five different characters each with a distinct voice which the translation seeks to emulate by having a different translator for each individual voice.

Special thanks to Nino Melashvili-Chokheli, wife of Goderdzi Chokheli, for giving permission to translate this work and for her guidance and assistance in translating the specific dialect used by the author.

THE TRANSLATORS

GEOFFREY GOSBY completed his doctoral thesis on Georgian linguistics in 2017. His translations from Georgian to English include *The Man in the Panther's Skin: A Condensed Prose Retelling* (2018), *The State Controller's Office of the Democratic Republic of Georgia* (2020) and *Life in Soviet Georgia: 70 Stories* (2021). As a member of the Oxford Georgian Translation Project he has already contributed to the translation of *Stories from Saba: Selected Tales from the Book of Wisdom and Lies* (2023) and is currently translating Sulkhan-Saba Orbeliani's *Journey to Europe*.

CLIFFORD MARCUS works as a translator mainly in the field of Life Sciences. His first degree was in PPE at Oxford and he has MAs in Italian and Classics from Indiana University. He has been studying Georgian since 2012 and been involved in several Georgian literary translation projects, including *Unlocking the Door* (2017) and stories by Goderdzi Chokheli. He divides his time between Tallinn, Estonia and Oxford, England.

OLLIE MATTHEWS began learning Georgian whilst reading French and Russian at Jesus College, Oxford. He has been a member of the Oxford Georgian Translation Project since its inception. His translations have appeared in *Unlocking the Door* (2017) and *Stories from Saba: Selected Fables from the Book of Wisdom and Lies* (2023). He is currently working on Aka Morchiladze's *Santa Esperanza*. Ollie lives in Manchester.

MARGARET MILLER began studying Georgian while reading History at St Anne's College, Oxford and joined the Oxford Georgian Translation Project in 2018. She contributed to *Stories from Saba: Selected Fables from the Book of Wisdom and Lies* (2023). She is currently working on an anthology of Georgian poetry and Aka Morchiladze's novel *Santa Esperanza* with other members of the Oxford Georgian Translation Project.

WALKER THOMPSON read Russian and German as an undergraduate at Magdalen College, Oxford, before going on to obtain a Master's in Syriac Studies at Wolfson College. From 2019-2024, he worked in various capacities at the Institute for Slavic Studies of Heidelberg University, where he completed his doctorate in Slavic Philology in March 2024. He has been actively involved in translation projects at Oxford since 2016 and is a contributor to the Georgian-English translation of *Unlocking the Door* (2017).

GODERDZI CHOKHELI
(an Unacknowledged Saint)
by
LEVAN BERDZENISHVILI

Under any normal progression of events, the Georgian author, screenwriter, film director, poet, and simply put extraordinary human being, Goderdzi Chokheli, should still be with us today; it was an abnormal progression that events followed though, and we lost this uncommon genius in 2007.

A significant number of us in the Georgian population have found ourselves the recipients of a hybrid fate: we lived in the Soviet Union and now live in an independent Georgia. Goderdzi Chokheli was the only one among us for whom this hybridity did not exist, for he never lived in the Soviet Union, but was instead like the hero of a fantasy novel sent back to the Soviet Union from the future—a secret service agent dispatched from independent Georgia to the Georgian Soviet Socialist Republic.

The Soviet Union cast the mould of the Georgian writer, whose hallmark was not talent but compromise. Mikheil Javakhishvili compromised when he rewrote Arsena of

Marabda in accordance with the resolutions of the Communist Party. Konstantine Gamsakhurdia compromised when, following his best novel, *The Moon Snatchers*, he wrote a three-volume work on Stalin; the list goes on. When the time of 'perestroika' arrived and Soviet writers brought forth their masterpieces from their desk drawers, Georgia's drawers revealed themselves to be empty: nothing written by Georgian writers had been unpublishable. No Georgian Bulgakov who had written a novel of the kind that would be published decades later had been born.

Goderdzi Chokheli turned out to be virtually the only writer who had written without compromise. He was Georgian literature's enigmatic phenomenon—an example of how a person could be so original that it was difficult for anybody to banish them. He conquered all with his almost childlike honesty and originality.

It is no surprise that the same criticisms were levelled at him that were directed at Vazha Pshavela in his time: "Who do you think you are, man, with your naïve poems, stories, and views? We are master craftsmen and have to compromise—why should you be any different?!" He was indeed, an entirely different man...

He has a small sketch titled *Nine Questions about Love*, in which the main literary trend is the reinvention of the fictitious world with the help of entirely real people. Characters who really exist talk with him like they do in the novels of future Nobel laureate Svetlana Alexievich. Goderdzi Chokheli intuited this trend far earlier; he set literature to actual voices.

In form he was the most modern of Georgian writers, while in content, he plumbed the pre-Christian depths of the

Georgian subconscious. His films enjoyed success throughout the world precisely due to their unimaginable originality. He was a modern-day mythographer. Incidentally, ancient Greek mythology does not give us myths of the same kind; Greek myths were plastic, beautiful myths, while mythos with Goderdzi Chokheli is of a non-plastic character. Non-plastic, painful myths and the naivety of their characters created a literature of the tragedy of our way of life which the censor was unable to ban because, by the criteria of censorship, there was nothing there to ban. Goderdzi Chokheli did not write anti-Soviet literature, he wrote non-Soviet literature. This is something that nobody else was able to do.

Georgian society was unable to fully accept this. As a person, he was alone: not a Soviet man.

His most powerful artistic weapon was his natural combination of the dead with the living. Their principal arena was his novel *Human Sadness*, which gave us one of the most important signs of our time. Its author showed us what a treasure each and every person is and the wealth that they possess.

Goderdzi Chokheli has a small masterpiece: *The Communal Crow*, in which a conflict over a crow takes place between two men, the first of whom made the crow familiar with him, while the second lured it away with better birdseed. When the matter goes to trial, the judge demands 100 maneti from each man, then asks each of them to scatter birdseed, promising to find in favour of whoever's birdseed the crow follows. The crow flies over, and instead of making for the birdseed, alights on the judge's head.

I don't know how we came to deserve this strange pearl

PREFACE

in a time of soulless gadgets, this uncompromising proponent
of spiritual purity in an age of dubious but inescapable moral
settlement...

translated by Geoffrey Gosby

PROLOGUE

"If you don't have time, don't start reading."

"Why not?"

I am writing about a godforsaken gorge: Gudamaqari Gorge. I had long wanted to write a novel about the people of Gudamaqari, but never got around to it. Although I am twenty-five and it's only been three years since I started writing, it seems to me as if it has been three centuries rather than three years, and I am tormented by the fact that I have not been able to write anything decent about Gudamaqari.

Up until now, I had thought that Gudamaqari Gorge was a big book with innumerable short stories in it. No, no, something really is not right with me. I no longer see people the same way I did three years ago. Now every person seems to me to be a story and I try to find a title for each one. So if you meet me somewhere and start talking to me, I will imagine right at that minute that you are a story and I will seek out a title for you. I do not know what to put it down to: at first, only the people of Gudamaqari appeared to me as stories, but now anybody, of any nationality whatsoever, seems to me to be a story. If until now, only Gudamaqari has been a book full of strange stories for me, now I feel as if the whole Earth is one great book, illumined by the sun and the moon, in which countless living stories are walking about. Oh, if only you knew how glorious this book is! The stories themselves erect monuments to good stories; they are written by the unseen hand of their Creator, and then the book is erased, and... if only I knew what is going on with me! I suddenly imagine that the Earth is the paper of this great book which is called 'the World'. If only I knew where this blessed writer is, by whose hand this book is being written... or whether it has a beginning or an end anywhere at all. Or whether it perhaps has neither the one nor the other. The Earth is one piece of paper, while Gudamaqari Gorge is another, the subtitle for countless short stories.

"Me?"

Who on earth am I? Who could I possibly be?

"Perhaps I, too, am a story?"

Besides, what have I to do with all these stories that are happening around me?

Do you know what I want?

"What?"

"As I told you, I want to write a novel about Gudamaqari, so let me actually set about writing one."

Perhaps you can't imagine how greatly I am agonising: I can't help but write, but then again, what can I write about and how...? For one, I'm writing about things as they are, without leaving anything out, but I'm having a hard time getting started. Perhaps the Creator also had a hard time getting started with writing the book of the universe. How I would like to start this way and never finish... I want to speak about everything as I see it and experience it. Don't be annoyed with me if I don't keep to the order of events in my book. Order is not for me; it depends on the story, and stories may have such a strange nature that they never ask me what I think.

But you have had enough of me, haven't you?

What can be done about it? I couldn't find a way to begin, I don't know what to start with, how to put so many stories together. Now see here! At this very minute, looking out of my window, I can see three drunk stories walking down the street and singing. They've embraced one another and are staggering along. Let me start with something else... even though they won't give us a break: they are from the village where all the stories are mad. Recently, I wrote about that village and since then I have not been at peace... look! They've just turned the corner past my house. I know ahead of time that they are yearning for a fight with me. On the whole, I'm used to fighting with them. Not only them, but all my stories fight against me...

"What about?"

"About why I kill them in the end. I kill them because I love them. And they don't believe me: they can't bear death."

"No one can bear death."

"I can. I love to end my stories with death. Death adorns the life of stories just as the sun and the moon adorn the gloom."

"Don't you feel sorry, though, about your stories dying?"

"I do feel sorry, but I have this rule: I don't write about anything that I don't love, and I imagine whatever I love at the moment of death, and then I regret that I killed them and this regret forces me to think about life. Then the people of Gudamaqari come and fight with me."

"What do they say?"

"That we're still alive—and what are you doing slaughtering us?"

I tell them it's a lie…

"What's a lie?"

"Everything that people see and experience is imaginary and death is necessary in that it puts an end to this illusion…" Though why am I lying? Nothing is illusory, everything is true and life is very beautiful, whereas I am killing off the people of Gudamaqari prematurely. It may upset them, but what of it? If one day everyone were to kill himself, what would happen…? One day, one of my stories was borne away by the others to its place of final repose. It was hot; there were graves high up on the mountain and that's where they were taking the story. For some reason, everybody was looking at me. Earlier, I had killed this woman off and at that time she had resisted me, saying, "Why?" Now she had actually died and the others were looking at me as if it had been my fault. I was looking at the deceased and thinking, for some reason: "What difference does it make whether she died sooner or later? When I killed her, she argued so vehemently with me. Does it matter? What has changed since then?"

"Perhaps it does matter. Perhaps it does make a difference."

Though I didn't want to start this way; it's all the fault of those three drunkards who came along, fought with me and went away. They were staggering along so wretchedly and arguing so vehemently with me, saying, "Why are you writing about us? We won't allow ourselves to die…" But this isn't all that interesting; let me try to start a different way:

THE BEGINNING

The sun was about to set, and strangely, I had the urge to write. It wasn't yet dark in the room, but before beginning, I resolved to light a candle on the desk.

I lit a fire and held some candlewax up to it and peeled the sides off in thin strips with a knife to make them more malleable. Then I remembered that I needed a cotton thread around which to mould the candlewax. I looked around and when I couldn't find one, I moulded it around a woollen one. I went over to the desk and set about lighting the candle. However many times I tried to light it, it went out. The woollen wick wouldn't catch fire at all. Then I resumed my search for a cotton wick, but I still couldn't find one. Somebody shouted at me from outside. I went out. A Gudamaqarian story had come from Tbilisi to see me. We sat down. I immediately started picking a title for him. He had no intention of leaving; I couldn't have been listening in the end, since I didn't even hear him leave. And so I went back inside and resumed my search for something to use as a wick. Inside one chest, I found a pile of papers bundled tightly together with a piece of waxy thread tied around them. I did not pay attention to the papers. I moulded a candle around this piece of thread, lit it, sat down at my desk and began to pray: "O God, You great Author of the universe! Wherever You are and whatever You are like, power and glory be to You. I know that You found it difficult to begin: it could not have been otherwise. Nothing happens without difficulty. O what a glorious beginning You must have made and You endowed everything in Your book with such great goodness that it is difficult for man to fathom where it begins. It is as if it is here, but also there at the same time. It is also within me. Look! Three drunk stories are staggering down the road. It's in them, too. It's in the dogs, the cows, the water, the air, in the earth, too. You write so gloriously, about so many things and You write so freely... I wish that I, too, could write so freely, moving from one story to another as if nothing were the matter. You manage to preserve such regularity through all manner of twists and turns. Thus, when I moulded the candle around a woollen wick, it wouldn't light, since that is not how it is written in Your book: a candle whose wick is made out of wool will not catch fire, and a man cannot be a man if he has a dog's heart."

In the meantime, the candle had burned down and I went back to the chest to fetch some more cotton thread. I unwound a length of thread and then, for some reason, I became interested in the bundle of papers.

I read through several pages and felt a boundless joy when I finally realised that they told the story of nothing less than the extraordinary campaign undertaken in Gudamaqari by the villagers of Chokhi. My grandmother had been directly involved in this remarkable campaign and it turns out that these papers had been passed on to her because she was famous for being able to keep secrets. My mother had not taken part in this campaign. She had been ill that winter and my sister and I had been sent to school elsewhere because there was no school in our village. It always pains me when my peers talk about this campaign…

So this is where fate has led me; this is the place I should start from; since the records are all mixed up, I shall try to put them in order and to present them like this.

The records were bound in a thick cover with large lettering that read:

THE CAMPAIGN IN GUDAMAQARI

On the first page was a list of all the distinguished participants in the campaign:

1. Vazhi Gogi: Commander-in-Chief
2. Bibghai: priest (Flag-bearer.)
3. Sebai: bellringer
4. Samkharauli: warriors' historian and geographer (Chronicler.)
5. Kimbari: philosopher
6. Chaghi: writer for the warriors
7. Zinai: medic
8. Gamikhardai: worry-collector
9. Salome: secret-keeper (Responsible for hiding records in case of necessity.)
10. Shete: fiancé

11. Elenai: housewife (Baking bread, cooking meals, etc.)
12. Tatiai
13. Tashkentai } scouts
14. Garakhtinai

(In case of necessity to be assisted by Elenai and Salome.)

15. Sophiai
16. Katushai } criers
17. Martai

(They are to sow panic and confusion in the enemy ranks by shouting. They are good at shouting.)

18. Ketuai
19. Ninuai
20. Siduai } rank-and-file warriors
21. Tasiai
22. Kotoriani woman
23. Shirvaniani woman } intelligence section
24. Shijani woman
25. Kaltamze woman } marine section

(Since there is no sea in Gudamaqari, their duty is to maintain the link with the Aragvi until such as time as the war is over; until then, they must keep walking up and down along the river.)

26. Tebruai
27. Dariko
28. Lelai
29. Tamarai
30. Galilei

(They are to remain in Chokhi and look after the village, feed the cattle and poultry, and tend to bedridden elderly people.)

HUMAN SADNESS

Now, this is more or less the complete list of illustrious and valiant warriors and fighters, most of whom are women, since in the winter the men take the flocks out to pasture and the young people go to the city, and only the women and children are left in Gudamaqari.

FROM THE AUTHOR

Before I present the remaining records, I want to introduce the warriors of the aforementioned list.

1 VAZHI GOGI (COMMANDER-IN-CHIEF)

It's winter. The trees of Gudamaqari are plastered with snow. It's warm.

The houses of Chokhi village are spread out on the eastern slope of the mountain. Here and there smoke is drifting up from the houses. The sun took its time as it rose and spread its rays over the village. It's still quiet there. Not even the barking of a dog could be heard. Then one by one the older people who were still there began to come out of their houses. They let out the cattle, brought them to the spring and left them in the bright sunlight. The cows turned their cold backs towards the sun and basked with pleasure.

Vazhi Gogi came out of his house, wrapped himself in a bear skin and sat on the rooftop threshing floor, facing the sun.

Without haste, one by one, the villagers gathered at Vazhi

Gogi's rooftop. The latest people to arrive would clear their throats and sit down quietly.

All around is silence.

Vazhi Gogi is silent, too, and comes up with a new lie.

This is how it is almost every day: the old people come up—what do I know?—some of them aren't really so old, they are middle-aged, but most are old and that's why I say they are old. They are sad, partly because they never see their children and grandchildren, partly from the long winter nights and the heartbreaking silence. Vazhi Gogi is the only person who can cheer them up.

Vazhi Gogi fought in two wars and is very big-headed about it. A few medals always hang on his chest, and when the sun hits them, they shine so brightly that, looking at them, the Chokhians can't help but believe his lies. For all I know, they could be true, but as many times as I've heard the stories he tells, they seem to me more fiction than fact.

"Ah, sometimes a man's hard work isn't appreciated…" Vazhi Gogi began, in a heartbroken tone of voice.

The people pricked up their ears and fell silent.

"How much more appreciation do you want? You have those medals blossoming on your chest," Bibghai called out.

"Eh, what do you know? If my work was really appreciated, do you think I would be sitting here with you lot?"

"So where would you be sitting?"

"Well, there!"

"What happened, what do you mean by 'there'?"

"Well, for twelve years I was the captain of a submarine. For twelve years, I didn't leave the water. One day I'd be at the bottom of the sea; the next day I'd be somewhere else, eh!

HUMAN SADNESS

If you only knew what cities and countries there are under the water, none of you would stay here. You'd jump in the water this very day, but what would you get? Nothing, you don't know their language and they don't know yours… you wouldn't get on with them, you'd better stay here."

"Even if we knew the language, there's no sea here."

"Look up there. There's a lake up on Narianai Mountain. You could jump in there, its bottom is so big that it is directly connected to the sea."

"Is that true?" Bibghai asked, doubtfully.

"Yes, it's true. I'll have you know I've swum in that lake more than once or twice, though I could never put my head up because I was swimming in secret. Sometimes I heard shepherds talking on the shore, but I never brought my head above water. There is a city at the bottom of that lake, too."

"Do they also speak a different language?"

"Yes, they do. It doesn't matter. You'd better not go in there, or else you won't be able to understand their language, and you might not even be able to get out."

"Still, what language do they speak? How do they speak?"

"*Aiserio miserio miser*," said Vazhi Gogi.

"What does that mean?"

"Man is not appreciated as he should be—and it's true, too. Am I meant to be sitting here? What can be done? In twelve years I stuck my head above water just once and still they accused me of high treason."

"Why?"

"You mustn't stick your head above water."

"What did you say?"

"Get lost, you and your ship, too."

"Then what?"

"They put me in prison for two years. When they let me out, I started to work on a jet plane. It was so fast you couldn't even catch a glimpse of it."

"Didn't you have to stick your head out?"

"No. Who could resist the temptation...? I used to fly over our village, without even being allowed to look down at it. I would go, bomb some country or other, and come back again, and when I flew over the edge of our village, it would occur to me, 'Let me look down, maybe they're having a festival, but then again I stuck my head above the water and that was a mistake.'"

"If I were you, I would've looked out of the jet," said Tatia.

"I did look. That's why I'm sitting here with you lot," said Vazhi Gogi with a sigh, and then he went quiet.

The others sat in silence, too. Then the silence was broken by the deafening roar of an avalanche barrelling down Ozano mountain. For a long time Gudamaqari Gorge joined in the chorus of the avalanche, then everything went still.

Now everyone was discreetly watching Galilei, who was building snowmen on the rooftop of his house. Galilei had also been in the war, and ever since he came back, he's always playing war games. The chickens have got used to him. They don't run away, and even now he's surrounded by all the chickens of the village. He doesn't pay any attention to them, he's making snowmen, and nearby he has a saucepan of bread soaked in vodka for the chickens. The chickens are clucking. Galilei tosses the vodka-soaked bread; first, the chickens fill their gullets, then, when they are drunk enough, they turn on each other to fight. Galilei is the Commander-in-Chief. He directs the course of the war as he wishes, sometimes supporting the red chickens, sometimes the white ones. He always has a sword in his hand, waving it in the air, and shrieks at the chickens: "Tatia's chicken, attack the enemy from the left side and be quick about it! Treason, it's treason!!! Come on!"

Galilei shouts and the drunk chickens show no mercy. The battle lasts until the chicken armies fall asleep on the field.

"Who won, Galilei?" Vazhi Gogi asks the sword-brandishing Galilei.

"The colourful ones!" replies Galilei, pointing with his sword to a colourful cockerel that comes staggering to the edge of the rooftop. The cockerel walks slowly, with triumphant steps.

"Who are they?" Vazhi Gogi gestures at the snowmen.

"This is Napoleon," Galilei says, by way of introduction. "This is Alexander the Great, this is Hitler, this is Achilles, this is Shah Abbas, this is Tamerlane… they are all my enemies. But none of them will succeed."

Galilei marched around the snowmen, then he stood apart and shouted: "I'll knock your blocks off!"

He waved his sword in the air and then he ran at them. First he chopped their heads off, then he mashed them together. For a short time, he rested and then he screeched at the sleeping chickens: "Reveille, get up! Get up, all of you!" And he kicked out at some of the chickens. The chickens woke up and staggered around.

"Attention!" shouted Galilei and he tossed them a handful

of chicken feed. The chickens pecked it up quickly and stared at Galilei.

"Now let's go conquer the neighbouring village. We must exterminate all the chickens. You'll be in trouble if we lose!" said Galilei finally and he led the chickens away. They followed after him.

The women ran after Galilei, in an uproar.

"Where are you taking the chickens, you fool?"

"Get off!" Galilei shouted and gestured at the chickens to follow him.

"Don't drive those chickens mad, you crazy man!"

"I'll knock your blocks off!" shouted Galilei and he ran after the women with his sword.

Vazhi Gogi grabbed hold of Galilei, took his sword and tied him to a post with a rope.

"I'll knock your blocks off!" Galilei was yelling.

The women sat next to Vazhi Gogi, and Vazhi Gogi got ready to tell his next lie.

Bit by bit, it got warmer, and an avalanche thundered down the other side of the mountain.

Then the surroundings fell silent again. Only Galilei, tied to the post, was unravelling the silence: "I'll knock your blocks off!" He was threatening the women.

The chickens were surrounding him and clucking something to their Commander-in-Chief in their own language.

"Where are you people?" someone shouted from Galilei's rooftop.

"Help me!" yelled Galilei as soon as the voice reached his ears.

"Gamikhardai!" called Vazhi Gogi.

"Here I am, here!" Galilei was yelling.

Gamikhardai approached and from a distance started: "What's bothering you, neighbours, what's worrying you?" He was taking a knapsack from his back and taking out a thick notebook.

"Me first, me first!" Galilei yelled. Gamikhardai went up to him, opened his notebook and wrote:

WORRY NO. 1671
GALILEI FROM CHOKHI

"What's worrying you?"

"What's worrying me is that I haven't got my sword with me and I've been taken hostage!"

"Anything besides that?"

"Untie me this instant!"

"It's got nothing to do with *me*," said Gamikhardai.

"Untie me, or I'll knock your block off!"

"It's got nothing to do with me…"

"So what are you here for then?"

"I'm collecting worries, the villagers' worries, about all their trials and tribulations," Gamikhardai said and then he turned away.

"Damn you!" Galilei muttered under his breath.

"So then, folks, have you got any new worries for me?" and Gamikhardai went up to a group of women and jotted down the number of the next worry in his notebook:

WORRY NO. 1672
VAZHI GOGI FROM CHOKHI

"What's worrying you?"

"Same old."

"And what is 'same old'?"

"You know, just the same old thing."

"In that case, let's put down…"

"I stuck my head above the water, that's what's worrying me."

"Anything else besides that?"

"Did you look out of the jet?" asked Tatia.

"Yeah, that worries me too," replied Vazhi Gogi.

"I wouldn't worry about that, if I were you," said Tatia.

"Is there anything else that's worrying you?" Gamikhardai asked again.

"Nah, that's it," Vazhi Gogi replied. "Actually, come to think of it: *aiserio, miserio, miser*."

"Eh? What on earth is that?"

"It's a worry."

"Yeah? For who?"

"For the ones who live underwater."

"And what exactly is it they're worrying about then?"

"About the fact they often don't appreciate people as much as they should do."

"Isn't this a worry for those of us who live on land, too?"

"Yes, it should be."

HUMAN SADNESS

"Cheers! I think we've got a rather interesting worry here!" said Gamikhardai, and he noted down the number of the next worry.

WORRY NO. 1673
BIBGHAI: THE VILLAGE PRIEST

"What's worrying you?"

"You know what's worrying me."

"I know what *used* to worry you, but there might be something else worrying you today."

"I'll still build this house, but in order to do that I'll have to…"

Bibghai was silent for a short while, then he came out with the same old prepared speech that he had repeated God knows how many times already.

"My dear neighbours, who know that I'm not a liar, you are well aware, as is Gamikhardai, that this has been an ongoing project of mine for a long time now. You must let me have the village square on which the house is being built, and you must assist me in its construction. I don't want such a big house all to myself."

"How many rooms will there be?" asked Seba.

"I have planned for there to be five hundred rooms."

"Five hundred? What will we need five hundred rooms for, and where will we get all the building materials from?"

"We will get the building materials from all the houses we have: we'll demolish them all and build one big house in their place. We'll make it into a lovely home. Does it really make any difference? After all, we all want to be together. We'll have everything in this house. We'll even have a canteen with twenty rooms!"

"What would we need so many rooms for?" asked Tatia.

"What do you mean 'need'? We might as well go the whole hog."

"But that's *a lot* of rooms…"

"In the first room you'll take off your shoes, in the second room you'll take off your coat, in the third room you'll hang up your hat, in the fourth you'll remove your belt…"

"Will the women have to undress, too?" asked Salome.

"No. The women will only have to do it occasionally."

"What do you mean 'occasionally'?"

"Whoever wants to undress will undress, whoever doesn't want to doesn't have to."

"And what will be in the fifth room?"

"The fifth room will be the spoon room; you'll take a spoon and go on through to the sixth room, where the plates are kept, and so on… every room will be immaculate. When you get to the tenth room, you'll find the borscht. You'll serve the borscht and then go through to the eleventh room."

"What will be in the eleventh room?"

"The eleventh room will be the cherry room, but…"

"What do you mean, 'but'? It sounds good…"

"Yes, it does sound good, but maybe we'll scrap that idea."

"Why?"

"Where can we find cherries in the winter?"

"When we run out of cherries, we could keep something

different in the eleventh room?"

"Yeah, we could do, but it's bothering me."

"Does it bother you that much?" asked Gamikhardai and he enthusiastically brandished his pen.

"Very much," said Bibghai.

"Is there anything else bothering you?"

"The fifteenth room is bothering me."

"What is there in the fifteenth room?"

"In the fifteenth room there are strawberries, and then in the winter..."

"How many more rooms are bothering you?"

"The rest of the rooms are fine: in the sixteenth room there is *khinkali*,[1] in the seventeenth there are *mtsvanili*,[2] in the eighteenth there are apples, in the nineteenth there are tables—you will sit down, put food on the table, stuff your face, and then you'll go into the twentieth room, where the beds are already made, you'll lie down and sleep it off."

When Bibghai finished his description of the canteen, he looked at his neighbours with pride and asked: "So? What do you make of it?"

"It sounds good, but..."

"What do you mean, 'but'?"

"Wouldn't we have to demolish the old houses in order to build this new one?"

"Yes, yes. First of all, the old ones are useless; secondly, why live separately? Wouldn't it be better to be together all the time? What old house has a *canteen*? And thirdly, we need building materials."

---

1 Georgian dumplings.
2 Georgian herbs.

"Do you have any worries regarding the materials?" asked Gamikhardai.

"Not for the moment, no."

"What will we use for the roof?" asked Vazhi Gogi.

"We'll use sheet iron, which will start shining; it'll dazzle our enemies and blind them," said Bibghai and he looked at the neighbours.

"Let me go, or I'll start throwing stones through your pretty iron roof!" shouted Galilei, who up to this point had been quietly listening to the story about the canteen.

"If somebody lays a finger on that house, you won't be allowed in the canteen!" said Bibghai.

"I'll knock your blocks off! I'll only go into the cherry room!" shouted Galilei.

"You better behave then."

"Will there be a chicken room in your house?" Galilei asked calmly.

"There will be a room for chickens and one for donkeys."

"You know what I will do with you all?"

"What will you do with us?"

"When you have all finished eating in the nineteenth room and then gone to sleep in the twentieth…"

"We will go to sleep."

"Yeah, you will go to sleep…"

"We will go to sleep."

"…I'll knock your blocks off while you're asleep!" said Galilei, laughing, and he was very pleased with himself.

WORRY NO. 1674
SEBAI

"What's worrying you?"
    "Nothing."

WORRY NO. 1675
SAMKHARAULI

"What's worrying you?"
    "I'm worried because Gudamaqari is so far off the beaten path."
    "What do you mean?
    "I mean that historically and geographically it is a forgotten and inaccessible place. Everyone knows the Khevsurians, or the Pshavians, or the Tushians, or the Mtiulians, or the Mokhevians, but if you say you're from Gudamaqari, people would die laughing."
    "How come?"
    "Well, who on earth has heard of Gudamaqari? Hardly anyone knows that on Earth, in Georgia, there is a gorge, with the Black Aragvi flowing through it, which is called Gudamaqari, where the Gudamaqarians live; and that the Gudamaqarians are an ancient warrior race; and that of the

33

three hundred Aragvians[3] who fell on the field of Krtsanisi, the majority were from Gudamaqari; and that they were led by Ninia Aptsiauri from Atnokhi, and that in the shrine of Saint Mary they swore on the clan icon and from there they took their battle standards. To this day nobody knows that above Chokhi on the summit of a mountain there are the remains of a shrine and they called this mountain the Mountain of Monks, and that the icon of Mary was brought here from Akhaltsikhe during one of the wars... Gudamaqari, what a place! Now is the time for the world to learn about a valley called Gudamaqari."

"Woah, slow down, you sure worry a lot, don't you?" Gamikhardai stopped Samkharauli short—he was talking so quickly that Gamikhardai had a job to keep up!

Samkharauli stopped speaking.

WORRY NO. 1676
KIMBARI

"What's worrying you?"

"I have no idea where the beginning is."

"What do you mean, the beginning?"

"Everything we can see and everything we can't see."

"Have you just plucked that out of thin air?"

---

3 Refers to a detachment of troops from the Aragvi valley who fought the last stand at the Battle of Krtsanisi in 1795, when a Persian army invaded Georgia and destroyed the capital, Tbilisi.

HUMAN SADNESS

"What, you don't like it?"

"No, it's an interesting worry, but what's it to us where the beginning is?"

"Do you know where the end is?"

"The end is death."

"You're wrong. That's not true."

"Why's it not true?"

"Death is also a beginning, but not the main beginning. The main beginning is something else."

"God?"

"It might be God, but where is He?"

"Is that worrying you?"

"Yes, I know that the end and the beginning are one, that the beginning is in the end, but how is that possible? Where are they?"

"Is anything else worrying you?"

"Why would anything else be worrying me?"

"Galilei is tied to a pole. Isn't that worrying you?"

"No, it's not."

"How come?"

"It's not my problem. Galilei deserved to be tied up. Why didn't you untie him?"

"It's not my problem either."

"Untie me, or I'll take you into the twentieth room and knock your blocks off!" shouted Galilei, but not a soul was listening; there were only the chickens who started shrieking.

WORRY NO. 1677
CHAGHI

"What's worrying you?"

Chaghi was a young man. Up until this point, he had been sitting quietly and listening to the old men. Ten days had passed since he had come up from the town. He had already got used to the dull, dreary days spent up in the mountains. So far, the Worry Collector, Gamikhardai, had been avoiding talking to him, but then he wrote down the number of the worry and asked for a second time: "What's worrying you?"

"What's worrying me? Oh, nothing…"

"Nothing at all?"

"Nothing."

"So why are you looking so down?"

"How do I know? Maybe I'm missing the town."

"Is it because you're in love?"

"No, no, I'm not."

"So what's worrying you?"

"I've got to write up my thesis for my diploma."

"What do you have to write about?"

"Who knows? I've got to write an essay about Gudamaqari, but what is there to write about?"

"And so it's worrying you."

"Yes, it's worrying me."

"Are you really not in love?"

"No, I'm not, but even if I were, why should love

be a worry?"

"Why not? Love is the greatest worry."

"Are you in love then?"

"I was."

"Go on."

"When she was walking along the road one day, some bandits were lying in wait and they attacked her. She didn't say anything for quite a while. One day she was sitting and she looked up at me without making a sound. I asked her what was wrong. She didn't say anything. Then she came up to me and kissed me on the knees. I reached down and hugged her, but she pulled herself from my arms and went away. She went away and... that's all really... she went away. She threw herself into the churning waters of the Aragvi. And so then I turned to collecting people's worries. Any worry at all in the world, I have to collect it; and then go to God."

"What was her name?" asked Chaghi.

"Nino."

"Which village was she from?"

"Didebani. We buried her not too far from the grave-yard."

"How come?"

"Because she killed herself of her own will. The people were angry and nobody knew yet what had happened to her. But then the bandits started boasting about what they had done..." Tears started welling in Gamikhardai's eyes and so that Chaghi would not notice he turned around, went over to Salome, and wrote down the number of the worry in his notebook.

WORRY NO. 1678
SALOME

"What's worrying you?"

"Don't breathe a word about this to anyone else."

"A word about what?"

"About us building a communal house."

"Let them find out, so what?"

"They'll interfere."

"What else worries you?"

"It looks like there's a big snowstorm coming."

"Let it come, so what?"

"Big avalanches will come."

"Isn't there anything else worrying you?"

"My daughter-in-law is ill and I haven't heard any news about her children."

"Anything else?"

"Nothing else, so far…"

WORRY NO. 1679

As soon as Gamikhardai had written down the number of the worry, Garakhtinai rushed up to the rooftop, shrieking, followed by Tashkentai, cursing.

"What is it? What's happened?" Vazhi Gogi leapt to

his feet.

"Just this: nobody respects us Chokhians any more."

"How could they not respect us? Where'd you get that idea?"

"Here, Tashkentai will bear witness that I'm telling the truth," Garakhtinai said, and looked at Tashkentai.

"I'll not just bear witness, I'll do you one better," said Tashkentai.

"Come here, son!" Garakhtinai called to her wretched child Shete, who was huddled pitifully in the corner of the rooftop.

"You see this child here?"

"We see him," said Seba.

"We see him," Vazhi Gogi agreed.

"Hey, everyone, you all see him, don't you?" Garakhtinai called loudly.

"I'll knock your blocks off!" Galilei joined in.

"Shut up, you!" Vazhi Gogi barked at him.

"I'll sort you out in the twentieth room," Galilei threatened.

"You see him?" shouted Garakhtinai.

"We do!" the people replied.

"You see Chokhi's shrine of St George?"

"We see it. May we all receive his blessing!"

"Wasn't it the law in Gudamaqari that any son of Chokhi's St George, even if he was blind or lame, could knock on any door and ask for a woman's hand in marriage, without being refused?"

"Yes, that's true! That's true!" said the priest, jumping to his feet.

"Then what?"

"What then?"

"Then this: it's no longer so."

"How come?"

"You see my child here? Come over here, son." Garakhtinai dragged Shete, still miserably hunched over, towards herself and then asked: "Do you want a wife?"

"Yes," said Shete.

"Hear that, he does…"

"Then what?"

"Then this: they didn't give us one."

"Who didn't give you a woman? Who refused?"

"Mtsaria from Didebani village, that's who."

"What?"

"He said, 'I won't give her to you. It's a different time now. Wake up, eh! You're living in the Dark Ages.' "

"The Dark Ages?"

"Did he really say that?"

"Yes, and even more: 'I won't give her to you. It used to be the law, but it's not any more.' "

"Do you want this woman with all your heart, son?" the priest asked Shete.

"Yes, I do."

"Come, make your petition in the shrine." The priest brought Shete over to the shrine and the others followed, indignant and troubled.

"Untie me, damn you!" roared Galilei, but nobody took any notice. They all gathered below the icon, kneeling by the boundary stone.

Gamikhardai went up to Garakhtinai and wrote down

her worry.

"What worries you?"

"Leave me alone, my dear Gamikardhai!"

"Tell me what is worrying you."

"I feel like my heart could give out at any moment and you're still carrying on like this..."

"You tell me, then." Now he turned to Tashkentai.

"What worries me is that, from this day on, Chokhi villagers are losing their privileges in Gudamaqari Gorge. Today, the villagers of Didebani refused us, tomorrow it will be the villagers from Gamsi and the ones from Chobolaurni the day after."

"Tashkentai is right!" the people cried here and there.

"We must take the clan icon out and go on a procession round the village, so that nobody will dare to refuse us again," said Vazhi Gogi.

The people seemed to like this idea, and they shouted up at the priest above them (since they were down by the boundary stone, they couldn't go any further up): "Bring the clan icon, Bibghai!"

"Never! Over my dead body," Bibghai shouted down.

Then Vazhi Gogi, Sebai and Samkharauli got up and negotiated with the priest, saying now is the time to frighten the people of Gudamaqari, to regain the old privileges in the other villages.

THE CLAN ICON

Gudamaqari Gorge was first settled by the Chokhians, who called their village Chokhi. This was before the arrival of Christianity, and the Chokhians too were idolaters, although when they adopted Christianity, they recognised the lunar deity—St George—as their chief figure of worship.

Gudamaqari Gorge gradually began to see new villages appear. Those who had fled from their sworn enemies in Khevsureti took cover in that inaccessible place and made it their home as well. They erected their own shrines.

St George was divided up into three hundred and sixty-three pieces, and the Chokhians' part of St George is the tongue. For that reason, the people of Gudamaqari were wary of "falling victim to the Chokhians' tongue".

The Chokhians arranged for a goldsmith to forge them an icon, and brought it down into the newly built villages of Gudamaqari Gorge.

Whichever village they entered, they would first ring bells, then make the people of the village swear their obedience to the Chokhians on the icon. This obedience consisted essentially in the bearers of other names recognising the supremacy of the Chokhian name, and if a Chokhian came to them to ask for the hand of one of their women, in their not refusing, even if the husband-to-be was lame or blind.

That rule had been passed down from that day to the present one, but today it had been violated for the first time in

42

centuries, and this so concerned the Chokhians that even the women were no longer able to hide their concern, and they asked for the clan icon to be borne out.

The icon was entrusted with another mission as well: if the enemy arrived at Georgia's gates, they would bring the icon down into Gudamaqari, and whoever was able to was to follow the icon party; it had last been kissed by three hundred Aragvians on the road to Krtsanisi.

"Bring down the icon, we will swear too that we will either restore our rights, or not one of us will return!" the women cried to the priest, who indeed brought the icon down and jingled the bells that adorned the processional banner.

That night, the Chokhians held a gathering in Vazhi Gogi's reception hall. The majority were women, and such a hubbub was issuing forth from them that nothing else could be heard.

They decided to wage a campaign in Gudamaqari the very next day. They wrote down a list of warriors and assigned their roles to them in accordance with the proper rules and procedure.

The assembled Chokhians unanimously appointed Vazhi Gogi their Commander-in-Chief, and entrusted the formation of the army to him.

"We must henceforth arrange everything so that nothing more will hinder us," Vazhi Gogi said, and explained to the women what he meant.

"No distinguished campaign has ever been waged blindly and in disorder," Vazhi Gogi said. "When going to make war on another country, every great Commander-in-Chief would take with them writers, philosophers, historians, and geographers. This firstly emphasised their status as figures of culture, and we certainly aren't entirely backward. These people are also necessary, firstly so that the foe can see what an educated breed they are dealing with, and secondly, so that they can be of benefit to us. Our philosophers, writers, and historians will record many things about those people whom we shall make swear an oath upon the icon. These records will then be of who can tell what use to our children and grandchildren. And if they are not of any use, will they have done any harm? Also, if we make records of different things, by doing so we will confound the enemy and make them submit all the more. First of all, it is necessary for us to appoint a historian and geographer; this is essential. A historian is just as essential for this campaign as a Commander-in-Chief. If I am not mistaken, we must appoint Samkharauli as the historian-geographer and chronicler. Stand, Samkharauli!

Samkharauli stood.

"Are you in favour?"

"We are," they called out from here and there.

"I think that we should take Chaghi as the campaign writer," the Worry Collector said.

Chaghi refused at first, and was generally against the campaign. He tried very hard to convince the women that they were doing something foolish, and that Mtsaria from Didebani was right.

"In what way right?"

"In that the girl is his to marry off to whomever he wants, and why are you trying to enslave and subjugate anybody?"

"What do you mean his? Why should he refuse us? When have the Chokhians ever been refused?"

"I want a wife, and why do they refuse me?" Shete, who

was hunched in the corner, shouted out.

"People, untie me, I'm cold!" Galilei's cry resounded from outside, and Chaghi went outside. A few minutes later he returned, Galilei following behind, who called out: "You'll all be sorry—I'll knock all your blocks off in the twentieth room!"

"Wait, Galilei, we agreed," Chaghi said, calming Galilei, and Galilei calmed down.

"Will you be the campaign writer or won't you?" the Commander-in-Chief asked Chaghi.

"Yes, you have to write an essay about Gudamaqari in any case," the Worry Collector whispered to him.

"I will be," Chaghi agreed.

"It will be your duty to write down events that happened; I'll write down philosophical accounts and also carry out inquiries," Kimbari said.

It was decided.

That same night the list of warriors was composed, and the Commander-in-Chief assigned everybody a place on it. The army was formed according to need and military custom.

Infantry were selected, as were criers, scouts, an Intelligence Section, and a Marine Section comprising two women; there's no sea in Gudamaqari, but they paid regard to customary campaign rules all the same and charged the 'Marine Section' with travelling up and down the Aragvi until the campaign was over. Several women and Galilei were assigned to remain in their village.

"What did he say? You aren't taking me with the army?" Galilei exclaimed, offended.

"You stay here. There's a lot to be done here as well."

"Which of you is a better warrior than me? Didn't your damned eyes see not long ago how many famed warriors' blocks I removed? Jalal al-Din, the Macedonian, Achilles, Hitler—didn't you see?"

"We saw."

"Well then, why are you shunning me?"

"You know that the enemy could attack our village while we aren't here, and who can fortify it?"

"You've got me here! I'm staying here!" Galilei cried.

"There's one more complicated matter," the Commander-in-Chief said, reviewing the ranks.

"What?"

"We need a doctor."

"We do."

"Well then, we have to bring Zinai along somehow."

That night they sent Galilei flying to Kitokhi on horseback to bring back Gudamaqari's general doctor. Galilei lied to the doctor that Vazhi Gogi was unwell, and that he was dying. They told the doctor the plan there and Zinai refused at first, then they frightened her, saying if she didn't follow them, they'd kill her.

"That's right, we'll knock your block off if you don't!" Galilei added, and Zinai too was won over for the campaign.

It was decided that night that the very next day, the scouts should send avalanches galloping down into the entrance to Gudamaqari Gorge, so that nobody would be able to enter it until the campaign had ended.

"I'll have trouble walking on foot; you'll have to tie a horse to a sledge for me," Zinai said.

"She really can't walk," Tatia testified.

HUMAN SADNESS

"Very well then, you'll sit on the sledge that carries our provisions," the Commander-in-Chief assented.

Nobody so much as closed their eyes that night. A battle plan was composed. It was decided that the village from which Shete's bride was to be brought forth should be attacked last.

"Yes, it's better that way; let's first make the others swear that we'll go straight to the wedding afterwards," Garakhtinai said, liking the general's plan.

They gathered provisions and each armed themselves as best they could. The best guns were given to the scouts. The scouts sewed themselves white dresses from calico so they would remain unnoticed in the snow.

They slept briefly for an hour or two at dawn, and once the dawn had fully arrived, the ringing of bells broke out.

The army awoke and gathered beneath the icon on a small meadow. All were ready to fight.

"Line up in height order!" the Commander-in-Chief ordered, and the women arranged themselves one after the other in a row. Some held a gun, and some a sword.

Sebai rang the bells. The priest brought down the clan icon. He came out and stood on the hill and called out: "May the icon show its wrath to whoever betrays the campaign!"

"Amen!" the women roared.

"Swear that you'll restore the old order!"

"We swear it!"

"Godspeed!"

"Amen!"

The Commander-in-Chief then gave the order to advance, and the army began its march.

FROM THE AUTHOR AGAIN

I knew all this by transmission and I've probably missed out a lot of things as well. For the notes with "The Gudamaqari Campaign" written on the cover, I shall try to present this illustrious campaign while preserving the proper sequence of events. There are five books full of these notes:

1. The Historian-Geographer's Notebook, on which is written *Chronicles* in big letters.
2. The Philosopher's Notebook, likewise bearing the legend *The Philosophy of the Gudamaqarians* in big letters.
3. The Writer's Notebook, on which is written *Human Sadness*. I liked that very much so that is what I called my novel.
4. The Worry Collector's Notebook, on the cover of which is written *The Worries of Gudamaqari*.
5. The Intelligence Section Notebook, on which is written *Intelligence Missions*.

The entire campaign is more or less covered in these five notebooks. I don't think there's any need to cover everything. I shall try to select the most interesting stories.

But wait, I almost missed something: alongside these same notebooks there are some letters, which the warriors sent to the inhabitants of the village, and several astute commentaries, which the Commander-in-Chief wrote in the field.

The promise was broken!

(from the *Chronicles* notebook)

The promise was broken!

This news spread like wildfire throughout Gudamaqari, and the Chokhians had to get the clan icon out. The whole gorge had to be subdued and the population had to renew their vow to comply with the Chokhians' demands again.

The campaign leader was an experienced Chokhian, a veteran of many wars, who had lived twelve years underwater, the popular leader, Vazhi Gogi.

Today, 6th February, the Chokhian army has headed east. The priest strides ahead holding the icon, the Commander-in-Chief follows, then the bellringer and after them come the rest of us, the historians, the philosophers and the warriors.

THE BATTLE PLAN

(from the *Intelligence Missions* notebook)

The Commander-in-Chief surveyed the Gudamaqari Gorge and decided to attack the following villages:

1. Chobolaurni
2. Lida
3. Khoza
4. Tsutskunaurni
5. Kotoriani
6. Nislaurni

7. Lagaziani
8. Torelaani
9. Pakhviji
10. Sachali Chala
11. Kichokhi
12. Lutkhubi
13. Dikhcho
14. Bakhani
15. Tsinamkhari
16. Makarta
17. Kitokhi

After Kitokhi is the village of Didebani. The Commander-in-Chief decided to take over Kitokhi, but not to enter Didebani. We will enter the village last after making all the others swear on the icon and Didebani will have no other choice. We'll slip past this village quietly and take the rest of the villages in the following order:

18. Gamsi
19. Chalivelni
20. Atnokhi
21. Boseli
22. Dumatskho
23. Sakore
24. Kakeeni
25. Busarchili
26. Salagho

After that we will attack Didebani with our main forces.

Scouts have been sent this very day to the entrance of the gorge to seal it up with an avalanche. And the navy has been sent up the river.

CHOBOLAURNI
(from the *Chronicles* notebook)

The village of Chobolaurni is situated two kilometres to the east of Chokhi. The village is crisscrossed by rocky gorges from both sides. The snow makes it more difficult to enter the village; it is hard to go up the trail; but the order of the Commander-in-Chief is firm: "The first strike has to be like lightning and we therefore have to use total force. The first victory must inspire the fighters and pave the way for further victories." Such were the words of the Commander-in-Chief.

The army is moving ahead. Snow and silence all around. The village came into view. The Commander-in-Chief brought the warriors to a halt, and because the scouts had not yet returned from the mouth of the gorge, he sent Elenai and Salome to Chobolaurni. The women returned within fifteen minutes.

"What is the news?" the Commander-in-Chief asked.

"The women are sitting on the rooftop knitting socks," the scouts said.

Our campaign is sensible for the very reason that in the wintertime, the men are out tending the flocks and that despite the fact that our army also consists only of women... but then again, they're *our* women!…

The Commander-in-Chief gave the order to attack and the criers rushed into the village with a mighty cry. The bellringer filled the air with the sound of bells. The gunmen fired their guns with a thunderclap. The village is under siege. There was a frightful uproar. I think that the enemy has submitted to us; our banner is unfurled high up on an upper rooftop. Now that's what you call an attack!

THE FIRST VICTORY
(from the *Chronicles* notebook)

The first attack ended in the first victory. Our army has entered the village. Our banner is unfurled high up on an upper rooftop.

The Commander-in-Chief and the priest are sitting on a couch. Our men have forced them to kneel down on the rooftop and they are taking turns swearing by the icon that they will recognise the supremacy of the Chokhians, above all when it comes to women. What can compare with this moment? The oath-taking on the icon was finished and it was the philosophers' and writers' turn. The opposition had to be confounded with philosophy so that they subsequently couldn't offer any resistance. The writers and philosophers are each writing news items of their own and the soldiers for their part are writing letters home. The opposition is stunned…

HUMAN SADNESS

QUESTIONS

(from *The Philosophy of the Gudamaqarians* notebook)

"Surname."

"Tsiklauri Solomoni."

"How old are you?"

"I'm turning eighty."

"What do you think life is, or where did it come from?"

"I'd say it came from God, as far as I know. When a child is born, the course of his life is charted by the position of the moon upon his birth. It is all determined from the very beginning."

"What is determined?"

"Destiny. A person's destiny is determined the day they are born. There was once a woman who was pregnant and gave birth to a boy. That night three writers came. The woman overheard them talking, they were writing her son's destiny… one of them said, 'This boy will live for as long as he can climb a tree, then he will fall down and die.' The second one said, 'No, let the water take him.' And the third said, pointing at a log on the fire, 'Until that log burns down.' Later, the boy's mother took the log out of the fire, snuffed out the flames on it, and kept it safe."

"And then?"

"The boy grew up, married a woman, and his mother told him about the log."

"And then?"

"One moonlit night, he was coming home from his flock. In the field he caught his wife lying with the neighbour. He slew them both on the spot, then ran home and threw the log on the fire. That night the neighbour's brothers came and killed him."

"If you had kept such a log, what would you have done? Would you have burnt it?"

"Sometimes I get so cross with myself, I probably would have burnt it as well."

"What is death?"

"Death is the work of God. He said, 'Let a man have two boys and a girl.' Then the Devil said, 'Who will worship you, if man doesn't die and lives forever?' So, as the story goes, God created death."

"When a person dies, where do they go to?"

"They pass on to the next world—so I've heard."

"What's the point of living a long life?"

"We love life, that's all."

"If God asked you how many years you'd like to live, how many would you ask for?"

"Ninety years."

"If He said, 'No, I will give you two hundred?'"

"I wouldn't be able to. I couldn't bear it."

"Why not?"

"Because of old age. I'll get old and frail."

"Do you think that the Earth will exist forever?"

"Of course it will! What else is it going to do?"

"And if war broke out?"

"Aren't we at war already, since you just attacked us?"

"I mean, if a proper war broke out?"

HUMAN SADNESS

"If war breaks out it'll be fought on the surface of the Earth, not underneath it. Why is the Earth called the Earth? Because it will soak up the war as well as the blood."

"If it just randomly flew away? Where would it go?"

"If it vanished into thin air, where could it possibly go? I have no idea. The water will sweep it away, but where will it sweep it away to?"

"Vanish into thin air!?"

"Yes, vanish into thin air."

"Can stones and trees hear?"

"They hear their own language, which is completely foreign to me. They have their own language to communicate in. Though I'm not sure about rocks."

"Where do you think God is?"

"Well… who is going to show me?"

"What is a dream?"

"The soul walks along, wanders around here and there—sometimes up in heaven, sometimes down on Earth."

"Do you think there are men in the stars or not?"

"People are up there and down here. We are in the middle, that's why we wear our belts around our waists: soul above, body below."

"So the people up there, do they wear their belts around their heads?"

"Of course they do."

"And the ones down below?

"Their feet will be tied up, so I'm not sure how they're supposed to get about."

"Why would they tie up their feet?"

"I don't know. When they bury them they untie them.

HUMAN SADNESS

They don't even put on a hat; they put it on the side of their head, on the right side. One person, they forgot to untie his feet, they buried him, and apparently, every night his mother sees him in her dreams: her child comes to her and begs her for help, because his feet are tied up. So apparently this woman dug up her son's grave and he really did have his feet tied."

"Don't they put hats on their heads?"

"No, they don't."

"But do *you* love life?"

"Absolutely, I love life very much. I grow softer with age."

A SHORT DIGRESSION
(from the *Intelligence Missions* notebook)

Before presenting the story from the Chobolaurni villages that is in the *Human Sadness* notebook, I want to tell you about a little message. In the *Intelligence Missions* it is written:

> "*The scouts who had been sent out have come back safely from the entrance of the gorge. They've sealed the entrance of the gorge with an avalanche. We can now act courageously.*"

I want you to know about a letter. As soon as they finished the attack successfully, the Chokhians dispatched letters to the village. Sending and receiving letters is the responsibility of the Intelligence Section: the Kotoriani woman, the Shirvaniani woman and Tasiai.

HUMAN SADNESS

WE WILL BE TRIUMPHANT
(from the correspondence)

"Hail, my dear brothers and sisters!

My greetings to you all. Your comrades-in-arms salute you. We grieve for your absence and kiss you on the face! I am delighted to tell you that things have started well. We made our first attack today. Chobolaurni has been taken. We are conducting philosophical and scientific inquiries. From now on everyone will be compliant.

Our victory is guaranteed!

The Infantry."

THE GREAT SPEECH
(from the *Chronicles* notebook)

When these philosophical and scientific inquiries were over, Seba rang the bells and the priest delivered a speech to the people of Chobolaurni: "You and we are peoples of the same gorge. We live below the same sky and the same Aragvi flows through our floodplains. Today, we have to be friends with one another again. If anyone from the other village has done anything to offend you, please tell us and we will help you. What division can there be between us? Nothing. Let us not conceal anything from each other. We, the people of Chokhi, have resolved to build a five-hundred-room communal house. To this end we are in need of materials. You can help us. You have walnut trees growing over where you are and they would yield very good material. As far as marrying women is concerned, you can marry off the ones we don't want to whomever you want. Today you swore on the clan icon, and oathbreakers will suffer the curse of the clan icon!"

"Amen!" the people of Chokhi cried.

"Amen!" the people of Chobolaurni replied.

After this, the Commander-in-Chief assembled his warriors and set out on the road to the next village, which was called Lida.

THE PRIEST
(a story from the *Human Sadness* notebook)

In Gudamaqari paganism and Christianity are mixed together. Even today, they bake bread in the shape of wolves, using clay for the teeth. They take the bread-wolf to the cattle shed. First they muzzle it with wicker and then they pray to it.

"May the jaws of the wolf that wishes to eat my cows stay shut!"

Then they take the muzzle off and break the clay teeth against the cattle shed: "May your teeth be shattered, oh wolf!"

"May your knees be broken!" They break the knees, and bit by bit, feed the crumbs of the bread-wolf to the cattle.

HUMAN SADNESS

Christianity was spreading strangely here. They were not yet completely reconciled to the new religion. But little by little, they began to believe in it.

The Catholikos summoned some villagers from Gudama-qari to Mtskheta and told them off, asking why Gudamaqarians were being buried without a priest.

"We don't have a priest," they justified themselves.

He gave them a priest to take back with them and advised them not to bury anyone without a priest from that day forward.

In Atnokhi, Akai Tamniauri, the slayer of twelve Kists, was dying. They brought the priest to him.

Akai died.

They could hardly break through the frozen autumn earth with their pickaxes. They had one man stand guard, watching over the grave to ward off evil spirits, while the rest, panting, brought the body, and before they laid it in the grave, the priest said a few more prayers: and once they got his permission, they slowly lowered the coffin into the hole in the frozen earth. Then suddenly, they grabbed the priest and threw him in, too.

The priest was shouting and trying to get out. But some frozen clods of earth fell down on his head with such force that he collapsed back onto the coffin, feebly. The Gudamaqarians set to work wholeheartedly filling the grave with dirt, mumbling to themselves.

"Dust thou art, and unto dust shalt thou return!"

"Dust thou art, and unto dust shalt thou return!…"

They finished their work, and a week later, there was something new to worry about: in Dumatskho, Gagilai, who had killed five Kists, passed away. The Gudamaqarians went back to Mtskheta and announced to the Catholikos: "One of our men has died and we can't bury him without a priest…"

"I already gave you a priest!" The Catholikos was surprised by their 'behaviour'.

"We put that priest in with another dead man, since you said not to bury anyone without a priest, but now someone else has died."

I don't know what the Catholikos said. Christianity took root in Gudamaqari. What could the Catholikos have said except: "Not knowing is not sinning." I think he could not have said anything other than this.

LIDA

(from the *Chronicles* notebook)

Lida is located at a distance of one kilometre to the east of Chobolaurni. The village is crisscrossed by rocky gorges from both sides; the road is more manageable and we go as fast as we can. The previous attack showed us that acting fast is half the victory. The scouts have only just come back and have brought with them the news that the village is nearly entirely empty and the only people left in it are an old couple with no children… they said the wife is ill and bedridden. The Commander-in-Chief is cautious; he says the enemy may be lying in ambush in some house or another and that we have to lay siege to them.

We encircled the village and began searching the houses. The village turned out to be actually empty; everyone had fled to the city for the winter. We carried out the main assault on the husband and wife and they, too, submitted to us. Our banner is unfurled high up at the top of the village of Lida. The priest makes the couple swear on the icon, and at the order of the Commander-in-Chief, the doctor gives medicine to the ailing wife. Seba rings the bells and thereby informs Gudamaqari that Lida is also the executor of the wishes of the Chokhi villagers, above all when it comes to women. Then the philosophical inquiry begins...

THE SOUL AND DEATH

(from *The Philosophy of the Gudamaqarians* notebook)

"Name and surname?"

"Batila Lidiauri."

"Age?"

"Eighty."

"Do you have any children?"

"I am childless."

"Where do you think the soul goes to after you die?"

"The soul? The soul is never lost, it gets separated from the flesh and it becomes like a dream. Exactly like a dream. The souls of the blessed departed shall abide in the Light, while the evil go to the Other Place."

"Where do you think you will end up?"

"Me? Childless people, apparently, are buried face down. But don't write that down."

"Why shouldn't I write that down?"

"A childless person might read it and their heart will shrivel up."

"What do you have to say about death? Do stones and trees feel death when they die?"

"When God discovered death, He thought, let's test death on a stone. While the stone was enduring his trial, all the other stones were so distraught that they fell completely apart; they could never forget the death of their brother, and they all crumbled into dust. God thought, this experience is not good for them, they are too weak for death, so He exempted them from death and then passed on to the trees, which suffered greatly; He broke off the branches of an entire forest, and they could never forget it. So then He exempted the trees and passed on to the water. The water couldn't cope, it started to dry out. Then God turned to man. Man cried and cried… then buried his dead and returned to mourning. Thus God allotted death to man."

A LITTLE SECRET
(from the *Intelligence Missions* notebook)

While they were in Lida, the scouts brought back a message from the Marine Section. The Sijanani woman and Kaltamze report that the Aragvi is frozen in some places and the ice needs to be broken to stop the villages on either side of the river contacting each other. Measures have been taken.

HUMAN SADNESS

WORRY NO. 1680
(from *The Worries of Gudamaqari* notebook)

"Name and surname."

"Batila Lidiauri."

"What worries you?"

"I'm worried that I will die childless."

"Nothing else?"

"What else is there to worry about, when you are alive and you don't have anyone to continue your line? What have I done to God that He has chosen not to bless me with a child, and that childless people must be buried face down?"

"Okay, that's quite a worry. When I go to God with my worries, if it's not the first thing I tell him it'll be the second."

SALOME LIDIAURI
(a story from the *Human Sadness* notebook)

At the top of Lida there is a rundown house. In this house, about ten years ago, Salome's parents betrothed her to Batira from Gamsi village.

Salome had golden hair down to her ankles. When she walked through the hayfields, you couldn't pick her out among the hay; the hay swayed in the wind and the girl swayed, too.

HUMAN SADNESS

Salome and Batira were madly in love, in their own way. Sometimes they would go months without seeing each other because they were so afraid of getting too close.

That spring, Batira's older brother was building a rooftop threshing floor for Salome's parents. Batira's brother was called Saghirai. Saghirai is still alive. He is a quiet man, subdued. Even if you spent a whole day with him, you would hardly get two words out of him.

At that time, Batira wasn't yet engaged to Salome, and they often met at the spring on moonlit nights. Salome used to go to the spring, fill the water jug, then after just barely catching a glimpse of Batira, she would return home.

One night, Saghirai waited in the hayfield for Salome on her way home and grabbed hold of her arm.

"I know who you were with," he said.

"What do you want?!"

"I love you, that's what."

"I don't love you…"

"You will love me—when you become mine, you will love me."

"That will never happen."

"It will. Otherwise I'll make both of your lives miserable."

That night, Salome couldn't sleep. The next day, she ran into Batira, but she didn't say a word about Saghirai.

Saghirai finished his work and went back home.

In autumn, Batira sent the matchmaker to Salome's parents and they got engaged. There was no limit to Salome's happiness.

Furious, Saghirai told his brother: "Don't do it, please,

don't marry Salome."

"Why?"

"Because, when I was working at her place, every night, she sneaked out to come and sleep with me."

From that day forward, Batira stopped going to the spring to meet Salome, and he didn't start making wedding plans with her parents.

Salome didn't know what to do, so she sent one of her friends to ask Batira what had happened. He returned a message, "I can't marry someone who has been defiled by my brother."

Salome went straight to the shrine and vowed that she was honest. Then it seems her parents tried to keep a close eye on her. They were worried she would hurt herself.

In Gudamaqari the Aragvi always runs black. They say that the villagers on the other side saw her going down to the river, taking off her shawl, tying it around her eyes and standing at the bridge. Everyone who saw her was so scared that they couldn't even think of helping her. It seems that Batira saw her, too. He couldn't run to help her either because he was so shocked.

The blindfolded Salome walked along the bridge. Then she walked back. Then she turned around to walk across again, and this time her friends appeared suddenly, screaming. Before she had even reached the middle of the bridge, Salome promptly jumped into the water. They say that everyone ran along the Aragvi, but nobody dared to go in. The water was roaring.

Batira ran and jumped into the water.

The Aragvi is black. They say that when he brought her

out of the water, her hair was flowing in the current like a hayfield in the wind before the harvest.

At the top of Lida village there is a rundown house...

KHOZA

(from the *Chronicles* notebook)

It may be true that there wasn't a multitude of people in Lida, but the priest still showed respect to those who were there and before he left, he delivered a farewell speech: "We, the Chokhians of today, are continuing and shall continue the customs of our forebears.

"A long time ago, we established a friendly relationship with the inhabitants of Lida. They would never refuse when we came to ask for the hands of their women in marriage. On multiple occasions, we have given assistance to each other and we need to help each other again, with building materials and with everything. For example, look at these walnut trees— they will provide us with very good building materials and, of course, we will not refuse such assistance, all the more so when we are planning to undertake such a grand construction project. A blueprint has already been drawn up and all we need are materials.

"You have sworn today on the clan icon and professed obedience. May the curse of the clan icon be upon anyone who breaks this oath!"

"Amen!" the Chokhians said.

"Amen!" Batila said.

"You, you say it too, madam!" they urged the sick lady.

"Amen," she whimpered.

Seba rang the bells. We took the banner down and set off on the road toward Khoza. The distance to Khoza is the same as from Chobolaurni to Lida.

The village was surrounded from above by a wood, but there was a large meadow stretching out before it.

The Commander-in-Chief sent the scouts out and they brought back the message that the only person in Khoza was an elderly woman who was fighting for her life and that she was expecting to die at any moment.

"How come she is expecting to die?" the commander said angrily. "We have to hurry up and attack and be as quick as possible to make sure that this person doesn't thwart our plans."

We didn't even have to lay siege to the village and within just about five minutes our banner was unfurled on an upper rooftop in Khoza.

"Where is the dying woman?" the Commander-in-Chief shouted to the people of Khoza.

"Here she is," they said, showing her to him.

"See here, doctor, make sure nothing happens to her while we are here, or else..." Vazhi Gogi warned Zinai.

"Kneel down," the priest shouted and the fighters raised their guns. They kneeled down and the priest made them swear obedience. They made the dying woman swear first, since it was more urgent. The dying woman regained consciousness and the philosophical inquiry began.

THE SOUL AND THE FLESH
(from *The Philosophy of the Gudamaqarians* notebook)

"Name and surname."

"Tamar Khozeli." (Dying.)

"How many years do you want to live?"

"As many as I will be able to. A person must live for as long as they can look after themselves. You shouldn't bother anyone else with your ill health."

"So will the dead come back?"

"You never wish your enemy to come back. It's all made up, all invented. We know the soul exists as much as dreams do. It's a lie when they say that a person dies and returns to the dust they came from. Then the soul exists no more."

"Does the soul accompany the flesh into the dust?"

"No, like when you blow into a wineskin and squeeze the air out, that's how the soul leaves the body and goes up to heaven."

"Doesn't the soul just dissolve into the air?"

"What else would it do? It goes up and turns into air."

"Does God exist?"

"I don't know. I can't really say."

"What drives someone to suicide?"

"Firstly, because they can't do anything anymore; they have work to do and can't do it. Secondly, life is tough; the Devil comes when you least expect him, and he tempts you with a way out. Then their soul stays with the Devil, and it turns into the Devil."

"Where are the devils?"

"Inside rocks. I saw them in a vision putting out a fire one night. And now people turn into devils."

"Is there anything you wish for?"

"No."

"How come?"

"Let me catch my breath a second."

The woman exhaled and died.

THE SEVENTH GENERATION
(a story from the *Human Sadness* notebook)

That woman, the one who has just passed away, was the last surviving member of the Aspaniani family. I don't know why Georgians have always had this curse: "May your seventh generation vanish," but it's always been this way. On rare occasions, they even cursed the family name, and if they did, it was always in this manner: "May your surname vanish with the seventh generation!" One way or the other, seven is not a coincidental number.

Seven generations ago, this woman's ancestor was well renowned in Gudamaqari, a strong man with lots of enemies, who was the blood brother of Kviria Kharkhelauri. There was no one whom Kviria trusted to shave his face with a sword, except for Butulai of the Aspaniani family. Kviria was never without his weapon.

His enemies bribed Butulai and once, when he was

shaving Kviria, he slit his throat and chopped his head off.

Kviria's half-shaved head rolled to the earth and shouted at Butulai: "May your name go on through seven generations of women and then vanish!"

THE SPEECH THAT THE PRIEST MADE
(from the *Chronicles* notebook)

"It grieves me deeply to see you in such dire straits. You have our condolences, all the more so now that you have once again sworn obedience to us. 'It has died out': that's what they will say about this family's name. But as for us, we will carry on our family line and we will become closer and show more support for each other. If you have any trouble, just tell us. Make a coffin out of walnut wood for the deceased. Walnut trees are generally only good for their wood."

"May the curse of the clan icon be on anyone who breaks this oath!"

"Amen!" the Chokhians roared.

"Amen!" the people of Khoza said.

"Take the banner down!" the priest shouted and the bell-ringer filled the air with the sound of bells.

The Commander-in-Chief gave the signal to go and we left the village without speaking. In this way, we paid our respects to them. After all, they had to know that we are a cultured and conscientious clan.

A LITTLE SECRET
(from the *Intelligence Missions* notebook)

The scouts brought some news today. The Marine Section has ascertained that there is a point where the river Aragvi has flooded. The flood waters there are apparently full of trout. Today a secret order was given to cover the place with snow and from time to time supply the army with the trout.

TSUTSKUNAURNI
(from the *Chronicles* notebook)

We came out of the gorge and the Commander-in-Chief brought the band of warriors to a halt. It is already midday. Things are going well. Elena laid the table for a meal. We started a fire and cooked a trout that had been brought in by the scouts. It is one kilometre from here to Tsutskunaurni. Some haystacks come into view. Here and there smoke is rising up. The scouts have left to survey the area.

The scouts have returned and reported to the Commander-in-Chief that the village is full of women. The Commander-in-Chief thanked them and ordered the writer to draw up a decree saying that they are to be rewarded.

We cleared away the meal and moved ahead into battle. We quickly drew near to the village and before long had laid siege to it. The criers raised a terrible racket, then the infantry followed and the gunners emptied their guns. We, the philosophers and historians and writers, followed behind the Commander-in-Chief. We went around the whole village but didn't see a single human being.

The Commander-in-Chief summoned the scouts: "Didn't you say the village was full of women?"

"We swear by the clan icon!"

"So where are they, then?"

"They were there and…"

"Did anyone see you?"

"I don't think so."

"Your work is poor. Revoke the decree about rewarding them," the Commander-in-Chief ordered the writer.

"It shall be done!" the writer said and tore up the decree.

"It turns out their espionage is very effective," the Commander-in-Chief said, shaking his head.

"Can we raise the banner?" they asked Vazhi Gogi.

"No, not yet. We don't want to make fools of ourselves, since we don't yet know what lies in store for us. We should strengthen our siege."

"It's better if you come out, or else we will set fire to your village because you are hiding!" the criers shouted in all directions.

"You have until the count of five," the commander shouted. He put hay on one end of a stick, set it on fire, stood next to the haystack and started to count: "One, two, three, four…"

"What are you doing? Don't ruin us!" a woman shouted and emerged from inside a haystack. Along with her, as many as twenty women came out of the same hiding-place.

"Do you see? Now that's a strategy!" The Commander-in-Chief was surprised and looked inside the haystack.

"Put your hands in the air!" the gunners shouted and got ready to fire.

The women raised their hands.

"On your knees!"

They knelt down.

"Swear on this icon that from this day forward you will not hide from us, that you will give us your women to marry without causing any trouble and that you will do something else for us as well," the priest ordered and had them swear one by one on the icon.

Our banner was unfurled on an upper rooftop.

The philosophical inquiry began.

TSERAMTSERALI—ARBITER OF FATE

(from *The Philosophy of the Gudamaqarians* notebook)

"Name and surname."

"Eliso Mikhas Asuli Tsutskunauri."

"How old are you?"

"I'm turning sixty."

"What do you think life is?"

"I don't know anything, leave me alone."

"Why do we exist?"

"What do you mean? God wrote it to be so. He gave us the breath of life and He will suck it out."

"But to what end? What's the point of giving us the breath of life if He's just going to take it away again?"

"God is in everyone."

"What was the best day of your life?"

"I can't remember."

"Can you remember a time you were frightened?"

"Once I was coming back from Busarchili at night and something behind me was making a terrible noise. I was with my aunt and it sounded like something was miaowing. I won't ever forget it as long as I'm alive."

"What did they say it was?"

"The Devil."

"Why didn't he reveal himself to you?"

"Who knows why he didn't reveal himself to me? He might have shown his face, but my aunt told me not to look back. It was no joke!"

"Has anyone else seen him?"

"If he looks round, he might reveal himself to you."

"Are you scared of death?"

"Why would I be scared?"

"Why wouldn't you be?"

"Because death is a debt and we have to honour our debt."

"Once you've honoured it, where do you go afterwards?"

"Into the darkness, where else? I will fill in my grave."

FATHER-IN-LAW'S JUSTICE
(a story from the *Human Sadness* notebook)

Martai Tsutskunauri was married in the village of Kitokhi. She married in the summer and in the autumn her husband took the sheep out to pasture. The other shepherds went out, too. Only the disabled men, the old people and the women and children remained in the village.

It's winter. It's snowing. Martai's father-in-law watches the snow falling from the window. It's his ninetieth time watching the snowfall. Last week the family's cow gave birth to its first calf.

"They used to kill newborn children," says the old man.

"Quiet, don't let the children hear," the daughter-in-law warns, and points to the neighbour's children. They are watching the old man intently.

"Let them hear, so what? You know it doesn't happen anymore."

"Who killed them, grandfather?"

"Their parents."

"Why did they kill them?"

"When the first child was born, it had to be sacrificed at the shrine."

"And now?"

"Now they don't kill children. They kill newborn calves instead."

"When must we kill this one?" the daughter-in-law asks.

75

"After twelve days. You can't kill them any earlier than that."

"It will be twelve days old tomorrow."

"Go to Ninia and ask him to chop its head off for you. The snow is so deep, I can't get up to the shrine."

Martai went to Ninia's place. He told her to take the calf to the shrine the next day and promised he would come up, too. The village shrine is up high, at the top of the mountain.

The next morning broke. It's snowing. It's snowing. It's white everywhere. Martai can hardly carry the calf up the slope. From time to time, she slips and both of them fall down. Then it seemed the calf could go no further, its front legs buckled and it licked at the woman's foot with the tip of its tongue. She carried it on her back and went the rest of the way up the mountain like that.

The shrine is built at the top of the mountain.

Martai put the calf down, and for some reason, she shuddered. "At least it's a calf I've brought to be killed and not a child," she thought.

It keeps snowing.

It snows.

The calf hunched over pitifully.

A long time passed, Ninia still didn't appear.

The calf seemed to get hungry, and it lowed. Then it licked the woman's hands with its small tongue.

The woman waited for a long time. Ninia still didn't appear.

The woman knew once the cow had been taken to the shrine, it must not be brought down again, and she kept waiting.

Little by little, dusk fell. On one side of the hill, a wolf howled. First one, then others howled back from the other side. The woman knew that she couldn't take the calf back and still there was no sign of Ninia.

It got even darker. The howls of the wolves came more frequently, too.

The woman lit candles, said a prayer, singed the cow on the forehead and stuck the candles to the wall of the shrine.

She didn't have a knife. She swept the snow off the wall and picked up a sharp piece of slate.

She pushed the calf down and cut its throat with the stone. The calf lowed.

The warm blood gushed out onto the white snow.

She left the head there, hoisted the body on her back and ran down towards the village.

The howls of the wolves were following her, piercing her back.

"Where have you been all this time?" asked the father-in-law suspiciously.

"He didn't come…"

"Who cut its head off for you?"

"I did."

"Did you light the candles, too?"

"Yes."

"What did you use to cut its head off?"

"A piece of slate."

"Go!"

"Where?"

"Never set foot in my house again."

The wolves howled even louder.

"I couldn't have brought it back, that's the rule and…"

"Cutting children's heads off used to be the rule, too. Go, get the calf's head, don't let the head you've cut off dishonour the shrine, then go back to your family home."

"I will go straight back home."

"Get the head first."

"There are wolves there."

"Don't be scared. You'll be able to handle the wolves."

"But I'm scared."

"But I'm telling you!"

Martai stood up and went to the shrine. It had already got dark. She could hardly find the shrine. The wolves weren't howling any more. The candles were burnt out too. She started to feel around, searching for the head. All she got her hands on were a few bones. She froze on the spot. She felt like her blood had stopped flowing and turned to ice. Then something heavy and warm jumped on her back and somehow the recent picture flashed before her eyes again: the calf's warm blood gushed out onto the white snow... all she felt in the end was that some unknown beings were competing with each other to tear her body apart...

Martai was from Tsutskunaurni... bodies usually compete with each other for existence.

THE PRIEST'S SPEECH
(from the *Chronicles* notebook)

The sun was sinking ever lower and we set off from Tsutskunaurni village in the direction of Kotoriani village. So far each and every one of the warriors is at his post. There is good news from the Marine Section. We are not afraid of anything coming from the air, since our commander has knowledge of air combat and knows everything that is going on in the air. It is two versts to Kotoriani. We rush—but what is happening? The priest has had the Commander-in-Chief bring the army to a halt.

"What happened?"

"I forgot to make a speech," the priest said. "Bring the army back!"

"It's getting late and we need to conquer Kotoriani by nightfall."

"It's not possible. I will just cut in briefly and then we'll be on our way," the priest persevered.

Vazhi Gogi sent scouts to Kotoriani and turned the army back towards Tsutskunaurni.

The women in Tsutskunaurni had gone back to their hiding places.

"Should I drive them out?" the commander asked the priest.

"No, don't worry, they will hear us there, too."

"Do you hear us?" Vazhi Gogi shouted to the women.

"We hear you! We hear you!" they shouted back at him.

"Well, then, let there be silence!"

The priest gave his speech: "Men and women! People of Tsutskunaurni! Don't think that we attacked you; we only want to be friends with you. We have to stand together as one. It is better for all of Gudamaqari Gorge to be united. Let us build one great house and live in it. We have already come up with a blueprint. If you knew what kind of dining room we'll have, you would start cutting down hazel and walnut trees this very day. What we need is construction materials—materials! The house is yours, as well, and not just ours. We are friends, so you must be loyal to us and give us your women in marriage and your walnut trees; otherwise, we will not be able to fend off the enemy from the outside. Will you be loyal to us?"

"We'll be loyal, we'll be loyal!" the women shouted in response.

"Don't decide on anything without us!"

"We won't, we won't!"

"Well then, farewell friends! May the curse of the clan icon be on anyone who breaks the oath!"

"Amen!" the army thundered.

"Amen!" the women shouted back from inside the haystack.

We then set our course for Kotoriani. On the way we were met by our scouts and they reported to the Commander-in-Chief that there were only five women and one old man in Kotoriani.

"Is it possible that they have a detachment hidden some-where?"

"No, we did a thorough inspection."

"Are you sure you didn't make a mistake?"

"We're sure," the scouts said.

"Draw up a decree to reward them," Vazhi Gogi turned to address the writer.

"It will be done," the writer said.

We went ahead at lightning speed. We somehow managed to conquer and utterly subdue Kotoriani by sunset.

By 'subdue', I mean the philosophical inquiry. If we

conquer this fifth village, I would say that our Commander-in-Chief is endued with a great talent. Until now, the world has never known a commander who was able to conquer five countries in one day. It is true that we have conquered villages instead of countries, but in numerical terms, if you compare the size of our army and that of the rest of the command staff, it emerges that we will have conquered five countries, and what's more, we haven't even spilled any blood and everyone is promising us servile obedience. How good it is that we thought up everything with the clan icon and the philosophical inquiry! We will use the clan icon to negotiate an armistice, frighten them with it and confound them with philosophy.

Five countries in one day... even though we haven't yet conquered the fifth, we are nearly there. The soldiers will lay siege to the village, and the criers will run into the village to stir up turmoil. The standard-bearer will run out onto the highest rooftop. Hurry! Hurry! Or else the sun will set and no one will be able to see our resplendent banner. What is victory worth after the sun has set?

The gunners emptied their guns. The infantry entered the village. All in an orderly fashion. The defeated people of Kotoriani are brought out of their houses and made to swear on the clan icon. They take turns promising obedience.

The sun is close to setting.

Truly a Commander-in-Chief such as the world has never seen. It is time, it is time!

The philosophical inquiry begins.

LOVE AND LIFE

(from *The Philosophy of the Gudamaqarians* notebook)

"Name and surname."

"Vasili Kotorashvili."

"Age?"

"I'm turning seventy-six."

"What's more powerful, love or life?"

"Life, for sure. As long as a person is alive, life is good and then comes love."

"What is life?"

"Life is when you open your eyes and you see the sun and the moon."

"Are you scared of growing old?"

"I'm not scared, but my knees are. But in my mind I'm as fresh as the day I was born."

"What about death?"

"That doesn't scare me either."

"How come?"

"I don't know. Maybe I was given enough courage not to be scared. When someone is at death's door, they're convinced until the very last that it's not their time yet."

"What scares you more than that?"

"Nothing scares me, I'm a tough breed. I don't know when I'll die, so what have I got to be scared of?"

"Do you prefer the earth or the air?"

"The air. Without the air we wouldn't exist, for the earth

couldn't sustain us."

"But without the earth we wouldn't exist, for the air couldn't sustain us?"

"It's true that without it we wouldn't be here."

"Do you think the earth will exist forever?"

"Where would it go? Of course it will exist forever."

"What if there was a real war?"

"It would still be around. Even during the Flood, when the sea reached to the sky, the earth carried on existing."

"Is God inside us or outside us?"

"Who knows? There must be something else out there—if not, what created the world? There's the sun and the moon and then there are people. Maybe *we're* the gods?"

"What are you saying? What makes you say that!? When the soul leaves the body, where does it go?"

"Nowhere. When we die, we become lost."

"So then our existence would be pointless. Why does God need us to exist?"

"Because we pray."

"Is that the only reason?"

"Why wouldn't it be?"

"But what does God get from that?"

"Nothing. He has to help me. He doesn't need my help."

"What good is His help, if after life we don't exist anymore?"

"As long as we are living we want to live well."

"But what's the use of living well when afterwards we won't exist anymore?"

"Who knows? Maybe we won't be here to find out, will we?"

"But what difference does it make whether we live for one year or a hundred?"

"You can't compare one year with a hundred years…"

"What's the point of a hundred years when afterwards you just disappear?"

"I wish the soul stayed alive. No, no, there must be something in the next life. What about dreams? Sometimes I'm in this world, sometimes I'm in that world… the soul never leaves us, does it!?"

"Does evil have to exist or not?"

"Well, if it didn't, then kindness wouldn't have any value."

"What is the best thing about human life?"

"When you are young and love somebody. When you spend good days together and spend the rest of your life together, that's the best thing in life."

"If life became too hard to bear, would you kill yourself?"

"No, I would not kill myself, what on earth are you saying!?"

THE FISHERMAN

(from *The Secret Diaries*)

On 6th February we decided to spend the night at Kotoriani. No one knows anything about this yet. We sent the scouts to the Marine Section, to inform them of our location. They brought back a man who had been tied up. The Marine Section had caught him by the Aragvi.

Before we started the interrogation, our Commander-in-

Chief took us aside and warned us.

"Just in case, if he puts something in his mouth during the investigation, hit him immediately so he can't swallow it. He'll have infiltrated the lines. They carry little bottles which they swallow and then that's it, they kick the bucket and we can't get any information out of them."

The commander went into the barn and ordered: "Bring him in!"

The scouts brought the captive in.

"Untie his hands. So, who are you? What are you? Where are you from?"

"I'm from Pasanauri, Merab Melikishvili, fisherman."

"Where did you enter the gorge?"

"From the entrance…"

"So, the avalanche didn't seal it off? So it wasn't difficult to get in?"

"It wasn't too difficult."

"Scouts! You can't do your job right. Is this what you mean by sealing? Writer! Revoke the decree to reward them."

"Yes, Sir!" the writer said.

"So how are we supposed to believe that you're a fisherman? Have you got your documents?"

"Yes."

"We need to see them."

The fisherman opened his breast pocket, put his hand to his mouth and placed something that looked like an ampoule between his teeth.

"Nail him!" the Commander-in-Chief shouted, but the prisoner was already down with an injured head before he could finish the order.

"Get that bottle out of his mouth!"

The scouts swarmed in and were just able to extract a pin from the captive's teeth. The commander was dumbfounded and when the prisoner came round he asked him: "What did you put a pin in your mouth for?"

"So where else am I supposed to put it?"

"What do you mean 'where'? I'm asking the questions. What have you got a pin for?"

"To do my pocket up so I don't lose my documents."

"There's something funny going on here," said the Commander-in-Chief.

The scouts took his documents.

"There's nothing funny. I'm just a fisherman."

"Who has ever heard of fishing in the winter?"

"I always catch fish in winter. I flood the river at the top and there are always fish there when it freezes."

"Ahah, so you know that secret, too? So now we know you're definitely a naval spy! Arrest him!"

The scouts tied the spy up.

"Shut him away!" Vazhi Gogi ordered and they bundled the spy into a basket they had brought specially from home. Then they closed it up thoroughly.

THE MAN WHO BECAME A SAINT
(a story from the *Human Sadness* notebook)

Mamuka didn't like to work. He used to come out to the wild pear trees, lie down under them and dream of the wind rising.

HUMAN SADNESS

His wife bothered him with curses, and then she ran away. Mamuka didn't worry about it much. He sent the children away with her, too.

A shrine is built at the top of the mountain, above Kotoriani. Mamuka had never been up there before and one day, he suddenly wanted to go up the mountain and look down from there.

He really liked the place.

"What would happen if I turned into a saint?" he thought to himself and he liked this idea even more. He went down to his house, took off his clothes, wrapped his body in all of his sheets and started up the hill, screaming and screeching: "I'm coming, my dear Lord! I'm coming!" he cried out now and then. He was carrying a lit candle in his hands. The frightened villagers of Kotoriani followed behind him. Once they reached the mountain top, Mamuka sat by the shrine and commanded: "Kneel down! I am your saint, and with the face of Mamuka, I order you to kneel!"

The people fell to the ground.

"Now get up!"

The people stood and crossed themselves.

"Go down to the banks of the Aragvi and carry back any beautiful stones that you find there. Quickly!"

The frightened people hurried down. They gathered the beautiful stones and brought them up to the top of the mountain.

"You call these beautiful stones?! Don't I deserve better?" Mamuka shouted and rolled the stones back down the hill.

"Now go down and get me the stones that I deserve, or I will wipe out your descendants."

The frightened people rushed off down the hill.

For an entire month, Mamuka sat at the top of the

mountain and entertained himself by rolling stones down the slope. If he didn't like a stone, he used to say, "The saint does not accept this stone," and roll it back down to the one who had brought it.

It was autumn. The weather got warmer. The forests of Gudamaqari were turning yellow. It didn't rain, nor did Mamuka lack food or drink.

Mamuka wouldn't accept any stone brought by Tsitsa from Kotoriani. Tsitsa brought twelve stones up the hill and he rolled twelve stones back down. On his thirteenth journey, he brought a crystal stone, hoping that at least this one would be accepted.

"It's rubbish," said Mamuka and rolled it back down the slope. He was sitting there, watching how the stone rolled. The people were coming up the mountain in a straight line, carrying stones on their backs.

Tsitsa lost control of himself; he grabbed Mamuka and threw him off the mountain. It is well known that, when a man rolls down a mountain, his body will curl up in a ball. Mamuka was rolling just like this. The people coming up from below thought he was a stone, and they were so used to seeing this that they ignored it and carried on up the road...

WORRY NO. 1681

(from *The Worries of the Gudamaqari* notebook)

"Surname."

"Kotorashvili."

"First name."

"Nino."

"What's worrying you?"

"Lots of things."

"Such as?"

"Our child got burnt the day before last."

"Whose child?"

"Our neighbour Marine's."

"Can't you tell me in more detail?"

"Of course. Can't you see the charred walls over there?"

"I can."

"A while ago the head of the house, Giguai, was thrown in jail."

"What for?"

"God damn the governor! He was always after Giguai's wife."

"Was she after him, too?"

"What are you getting at?"

"Maybe the woman was into him, too."

"Marine and Giguai had a little boy. She used to put him to bed and the governor used to come to her. The boy got older and she put him in a separate room so he wouldn't understand. One day the governor turned up drunk and the boy was there."

"Then what happened?"

"I heard that the drunkard started forcing himself on the woman. He was tearing at her clothes; the woman put up a fight, she was ashamed for the child—he was just a little boy. When he saw his mother in this state, he grabbed the ash shovel. But how could he use it? The governor went mad and kicked the boy out. The woman started crying. He locked the doors; she tried to get out to reach the boy; then the blackguard did his deed and left."

"What happened next?"

"One moonlit night she took the boy to Saqorne Wood; she took with her two ropes, one for herself and one for the boy. She hung up one rope then the other. Then she sat down, hugged her son, and started crying. The boy got scared and ran away from her. He told us that she chased after him, but let him go and went back. The boy went home.

"In the morning, I don't know who it was, but someone saw smoke coming from the house, I think it was Kanusha: she called out but there was no reply, so she went inside. She went inside and found the house was on fire. The boy must have started it. The fire tore through the building. I have no idea how."

"Then what?"

"We all rushed in straight away and pulled the boy out. Some people saved the cattle. Some of them exploded from the smoke—they sounded like gunshots."

"What happened to the boy?"

"The boy's clothes caught fire. The stupid woman had gone and left a bucket of kerosene lying around. We thought it was water, so... we burnt the boy."

"And what happened to the mother?"

"Well, we found her the next day... are you going to ask me again what's worrying me? What else would weigh on a person's heart?"

Gamikhardai made a note underneath:

When I go to God, if it is not the second thing, this will be the third thing I will bring up with Him.

HUMAN SADNESS

LETTER TO GALILEI FROM THE COMMANDER-IN-CHIEF
(from *The Letters*)

Greetings Galilei!

First of all my fondest salutations and a handshake from afar. We have fought our way through five villages and we are now camped at Kotoriani. Our battle plan is working. We're getting on; I'm sure I can rely on you to do a good job at your end. Don't leave the village. Take care of the old people and the chickens. We will send for you if we have any trouble. Until then, don't move. Let us know if the enemy invades.

Commander-in-Chief of the Chokhian army

Vazhi Gogi

GALILEI'S ANSWER
(from *The Letters*)

Never fear!

I've knocked Achilles' block off, I've knocked Jalal al-Din's block off, I've knocked Hitler's block off, so what can anyone else do to me...? I won't need you if they invade, I'll knock their blocks off myself. Don't bring Shete without Ketino.

Galilei

A NIGHT IN THE WATTLE HOUSE
(from the *Chronicles* notebook)

Nightfall. This has been a truly remarkable day in the life of Gudamaqari Gorge. Today our Commander-in-Chief discovered his own genius. Now it is time for the world to find out that there exists on the spine of the earth a gorge called Gudamaqari. If someone should then want to find out about life in Gudamaqari, let him come visit us, but before then I will tell him that we mostly live off our sheep and cattle and grow potatoes. Among the plants, the walnut especially flourishes here. Just now, although it is night-time, our priest went to take a look around the village and came back very contented because he saw so many walnut trees. After coming back, he was sitting and telling the people of Kotoriani about the big house that we would have to build in the future. He said walnut wood would be the best material for it.

The Gudamaqarians are walled in by very tall mountains from all four sides; the sky sits on top of us like a hat, with its own sun and moon. We have as many stars as you could want. The blackest river in the world runs through the gorge. We have a lot of other things, too, but listing them all now would lead us very far away and keep us from talking about the campaign. And so:

The warriors sat down around the table for a meal; of course, we are a civilised clan and we invited the people of Kotoriani to share in our meal. The scouts offered food to the captives. Guards are stationed around the perimeter of the village.

The Commander-in-Chief summoned Shete and asked him: "What is the name of your fiancée?"

"Ketino," he mumbled bashfully.

"You aren't opposed to it, are you?"

"No, I want a wife."

"The most important thing is that you aren't opposed to it, since, if our campaign continues like this, we will bring you your Ketino in three days' time."

Shete's face lit up.

Then we talked over a lot of internal affairs with the people of Kotoriani and because the army was very tired and would have to set out again on the campaign tomorrow at daybreak, everyone except for the guards went to bed.

NISLAURNI

(also from the *Chronicles* notebook)

Day broke. The bellringer rang the bell. Elena set the table and we had a little bite to eat. The Commander-in-Chief rallied the troops. The priest said some parting words to the people of Kotoriani. We took the banner down and moved out towards Nislaurni village. It is two kilometres from here to Nislaurni. The scouts went on ahead. After some time, they came back bringing strange tidings.

"The people of Nislaurni are dressed in black. The majority of them are women. They are walking up and down the hills and carrying something slowly and with great care, as if it were a coffin, but there is no dead body in it. How could there be when the coffin is the size of a matchbox?"

"Are they really carrying it so slowly?" the commander said doubtingly.

"Yes, as if they were carrying a dead person."

"I get it. If I am not wrong, they are carrying a bomb and they are afraid it might explode. They are dressed in black because they want to deceive us, but this is only a manœuvre and they can't fool us. Let us lay siege to them right now and when we have them under siege, they won't be able to detonate it. Well done, scouts. If not for you, they might have placed the bomb in our path. Draw up a decree immediately to reward the scouts," the Commander-in-Chief said, addressing the writer, and we moved ahead at full speed. Before the people of Nislaurni knew it, they were under siege.

"Stop!" ordered the commander.

They stopped.

"Lay the bomb slowly on the ground!"

"Which bomb, what bomb?"

"What do you have in that box there?"

"A dead body."

"Don't fool yourselves, what dead body could fit in that box?"

"Why, a mouse."

"What?"

"A mouse died in our village."

"And now?"

"And now we are laying it to rest."

"Are you mad?"

"Why? It's a rule we have. We bury everything that dies in our village. We are all children of God."

"What kind of rule is that?" the priest said angrily. "Who gave you the right to think up new rules without our permission? Now you have to swear on the clan icon that you will give precedence to the Chokhians, and that if we ask for the hand of a woman in marriage or for the wood of your walnut trees, you will not say 'no' to us."

"We wouldn't have said 'no' to you before, either..."

"You might not have, but you still have to swear on the icon. As far as mice are concerned, how did you get the idea of having a funeral for a mouse...?"

"We have this rule that we bury snakes, dogs, birds and flies. That hill there, it's for these wretches," they said, removing the cover from the mouse, and the poor creature with its puckered lips and stiff tail came into view.

The priest made the people swear obedience on the clan icon and then whispered to the Commander-in-Chief: "It's better to let them do what they want, whether that's burying their own dead, or discarding the bodies without burying them; let's follow behind them."

Vazhi Gogi lifted the siege on the funeral procession and we followed behind. They laid the mouse to rest in the earth that they had dug up in preparation. When we were done there, we led the people of Nislaurni back to the village, unfurled our banner on a high rooftop and the philosophical inquiry began.

ZITANDARI NISLAURI
(from *The Philosophy of the Gudamaqarians* notebook)

"How old are you?"

"I'm turning fifty-five."

"What is death?"

" 'What is death?' Ha, ha, ha. When you die, that's what it is."

"Where do we go to after death?"

" 'Where do we go to?' Bless you! We go to where that mouse has just gone—that's where we go, where else? We go into the ground."

"What is in the ground?"

" 'What is in the ground?' How should I know? In the ground there are snakes, worms, frogs, what else?"

"What is the soul like?"

"The soul seems to be something different at different times. Sometimes it goes here, sometimes it goes there. You know, it depends how it looks in our dreams."

"In our dreams?"

"Yeah, we see our dreams and it's the same with the soul, it follows us everywhere…"

"Will the soul exist for ever?"

"It will have its own time, then it will go and be completely lost, for everything has its own time."

"Does it not turn into anything?"

"It turns into nothing. Then nothing turns back into

something, and so on."

"Don't you think that we often repeat our life?"

"What do you mean?"

"Well, for example, do you ever get the impression that we do something and it feels as if we have already done it before?"

"Yes, of course. When we were taking the mouse's body to be buried recently, I suddenly realised that I had seen it all before exactly the same. And then you appeared, and I realise I have seen your army before sometime, exactly the same, although I don't know when it was."

"Do you believe heaven exists?"

"They say heaven is where the souls gather and come together, don't they? But I don't know what to tell you. The bones get lost in the ground and the souls go up to the next world. A person's soul is never lost, oh no."

"You just said that the soul has its time and then disappears."

"Yeah, that's right, it'll have its time in the next world. Everyone dies twice, doesn't everyone know that?"

"What do you mean?"

"Everyone dies twice."

"How come twice?"

"Well, the first time you die, your flesh dies, then the second time your soul dies, and then you are completely lost and gone forever."

"Does the Earth have a soul?"

"Of course the Earth has a soul!"

"Just like people?"

"Just as people lose their souls, the Earth loses its soul too."

HUMAN SADNESS

"Can the Earth die?"

"No, nothing can kill the Earth. Its soul will live forever."

"What if there was a war? Not like this one, we Chokhians are behaving ourselves in a very cultured manner—I'm talking about a proper war."

"Then it'll die."

"Yes, if it burns, the Earth will die."

TWO HUNTERS
(a story from the *Human Sadness* notebook)

It was just past midnight when two hunters came stealthily out of the village of Nislaurni and set off uphill to the ibex habitat.

They were both young. Both went along in silence. They walked until dawn without making a sound. At dawn they reached the base of the rocky mountains and sat down. They took their knapsacks from their backs and one took out cornmeal porridge, the other some slices of cold boiled meat. They ate their fill. Nearby, a cold spring was coming out from beneath a stone. They drank. Each had only a handful of water.

"Too much water buckles the knees," said one.

The other didn't make a sound. They put their knapsacks on and set off along the rocky pass.

One was called Gagi, the other Jarji.

Both of them loved the same girl, and this girl was called Iamze.

Jarji was thinking of Iamze; Gagi was doing the same. Iamze loved Jarji. Gagi knew this.

HUMAN SADNESS

Jarji knew that, at this very minute, Gagi was thinking of Iamze. Gagi was also aware of Jarji's thoughts. Jarji felt sorry for Gagi from the bottom of his heart, but…

One of them remained at the top of the rock. The other went around behind it and startled a herd of ibexes. Gagi fired and killed a mother ibex. Her kid didn't run away; it stayed with its mother and started licking at her eyes.

They skinned the ibex and went to a cave to spend the night.

That night the wind rose and drove the clouds to Gudam-aqari Gorge. It got dark. The cave was lit by the fire. The kid looked into the cave from the entrance once, then ran away. The ibex's innards were sizzling pleasantly on the embers and the scent of barbecued meat was mingling with the clean air. The hunters were sitting there, still silent.

By the entrance of the cave, there was a thistle with a blue blossom. The wind was blowing and swaying it back and forth.

"You see how high it's grown?" said Jarji.

"What?" asked Gagi.

"The thistle."

Gagi put a bullet in his gun and smiled. Then he said to Jarji: "If I killed you now, no one would know."

"What wouldn't they know?" Jarji laughed.

"That I had killed you," Gagi smiled.

"You see that thistle over there?"

"I see it."

"I would make that thistle say that you killed me."

Gagi laughed and took the bullet out of the gun.

Jarji put wood on the fire and skewered some meat on a

stick. He had his back turned to Gagi.

Suddenly the gun thundered and Jarji fell on his face into the fire.

First, Gagi turned over the dead body. Then he closed Jarji's eyes and crossed his hands over his chest.

The wind blew and the blue-blossoming thistle swayed back and forth at the entrance of the cave all night.

At dawn, the sky got clear. The white glaciers cut through the darkness.

Gagi hefted the dead body and took it up the mountain. He carried it on his back until midday. When he reached the glaciers, he hid the body in a big crevice in the ice. He covered it with stones, then ice.

For five days, he wandered the rocky mountains. Each night, he stayed in the cave. Then he went back home, bringing the dead ibex with him.

"Where is Jarji?" people asked.

"Hasn't he come back?!" he was surprised.

"No," they said.

"It's been three days since Jarji left for home. He brought a dead ibex back with him. I was tempted to stay and follow the herd," he said, and dropping the ibex, he went back to search for Jarji. Jarji's brothers also went back with him. A few times, they walked around right above the place where he had hidden the body.

They couldn't find him anywhere.

Fifteen years later, in Nislaurni village, at the end of autumn, beginning of winter, a man and a woman are threshing hay with the oxen.

The man is Gagi and the woman is his wife, Iamze. Gagi

is already middle-aged.

Then man and wife spread their felt cloaks over the straw and lie down to sleep. At the entrance of the threshing floor, a thistle had grown, and the wind sways it back and forth.

The man laughed.

"Why are you laughing?" asked his wife.

"No reason," said Gagi.

The wife insisted, "Tell me, why did you laugh?" Gagi didn't say anything. That night, his wife wouldn't let him rest. Gagi thought, "She's my wife, it's been fifteen years, so what, I will tell her."

"You see that thistle over there?"

"I see it," said his wife.

"That's what I laughed at. Jarji told me, 'If you killed me, I would make that thistle say that you killed me.' That's why I laughed. What can a thistle say?"

The next morning, he didn't find his wife next to him. From above the rooftop he heard the sound of footsteps. He looked up. He caught a glimpse of Jarji's brother.

That very moment, a gun thundered and before he completely left behind all earthly vision, one last time, he glimpsed the thistle in the entrance of the threshing floor.

The wind was blowing and swaying the thistle back and forth.

AN UNPRECEDENTED ATTACK
(from the *Chronicles* notebook)

After we finished the philosophical inquiry in Nislaurni and the priest made a friendly address to the Nislaurians, the Commander-in-Chief assembled the troops, and on that day, we began an unprecedented campaign.

History may well never have seen another commander who took over ten countries in one day, and that as sensibly as we did. Other campaigns have left famine, bloodshed, massacres, ruin and humiliated nations in their wake... we, on the other hand, acted bloodlessly, peacefully and philosophically. In saying farewell, the priest always gave a friendly speech and from time to time touched upon the matter of the walnut wood.

By sunset on 7th February, we had conquered ten villages and made them swear on the icon, we had written down countless worries, had conducted the philosophical inquiry and so on... and in conquering the villages one by one, we reasserted our rights over them.

At sundown, we were on the approach to Makarta village and the rays of the sun no longer illumined our banner at the head of the village, yet we unfurled it anyway. By nightfall, Makarta had submitted to us and we spent that same night in a great philosophical and scientific inquiry.

At daybreak, we set out for Kitokhi. At the outskirts of Kitokhi, the Commander-in-Chief brought us to a halt and addressed us: "We have carried out an unprecedented attack. Each one of you is deserving of praise. Someday I will take you to the underwater cities, but until then we have a great deed to accomplish. The main thing is we have to conquer Kitokhi now and Gudamaqari is ours. In comparison with other villages, Kitokhi is a cultured village and civilised people live there and there is a school there. I know from experience that, while we have treated the uneducated villages thus far in a civilised manner, we must, on the contrary, treat the educated ones in a savage manner in order to subdue them. Civilised people are afraid of savagery, so here you are, let's go attack with total savagery!"

The criers ran ahead shouting.

The rumble of the guns began.

We laid siege to the village. We set fire to haystacks here and there, and within exactly one hour, our priest was making the kneeling Kitokhians swear an oath on the clan icon.

Then we began the philosophical inquiry in order to compensate for our savagery.

The priest made up his mind that he wanted to have a look around the school.

"We need to know what the children are being taught in school," he said and called the Commander-in-Chief over.

"Should we bring the army over?" Vazhi Gogi asked.

"No, don't bring the army into the school; lead them out in front of the school so the children can see and feel our strength," the priest said.

The priest entered the classroom and asked the teacher: "Are you inculcating the children with loyalty to the Chokhians?"

"Yes," the teacher said.

"Could we please test the philosophical level of you and your pupils?"

"Yes, you may."

The inquiry began.

From the window, we could see Vazhi Gogi leading the army back and forth.

THE PUPIL KOBA

(from *The Philosophy of the Gudamaqarians* notebook)

"How old are you?"

"I'm turning eleven."

"What do you love above all?"

"I don't know, everything…"

"If somebody told you that you could turn into something for a day and then we turned you back into your normal self, what would you turn into?"

"A cuckoo."

"Why would you want to become a cuckoo?"

"Cuckoos are good. They herald the spring and all day long they fill everything around them with joy."

"So you wouldn't turn into a fish?"

"No."

"Why not?"

"If I turned into a fish on land, then before I got to the water I would die."

"You wouldn't turn into a flower then, Koba?"

"No."

"Why not?"

"Somebody would pick me and then I would die."

"Would you want to be a horse?"

"No, I wouldn't want to be a horse either, people would sit on me and wear me out by making me gallop."

"Would you like to turn into the Aragvi?"

"No. Something would fall into me and I would end up drowning it. I would be constantly flowing and who knows where I would end up? That's enough questions now."

"Okay, let's finish. What would the teacher tell us?"

"What about?" said the teacher.

"What is life?"

"Life is when you achieve your goal."

"That's right," said the priest.

"That's the life we all should lead."

THE LONG ATTACK

(from the *Chronicles* notebook)

I ought to note that the Kitokhians were awed by us and vowed us eternal obedience. They liked our clan icon so much that they were saying oaths to it every minute.

From Kitokhi, we undertook a long attack. We skirted around Didebani village; this was a military manœuvre: we had to make a triumphal entrance and return home with the bride.

The scouts are working well. Good news is coming from

the Marine Section, too. The prisoner has accepted his fate. He hasn't given in yet, but he will. It's possible that he'll come over to our side. We are acting so shrewdly; if he has any brains, he'll choose to be with us. We conquered Lagheni and Sakore and we are now headed towards Busarchili.

By sundown, our banner was unfurled on top of a high tower in Busarchili. The oath-taking and afterwards the philosophical and scientific inquiry began.

GIGIA BUBUNAURI'S BLOOD BROTHER
(a story from the *Human Sadness* notebook)

It's snowing.

A pale stillness is settled on the slope of Busarchili. Only snowflakes rustle, quietly, quietly, quietly, like blessings from the sky. Then the cry of an eagle echoes: once, twice, three times. The eagle falls silent and the stillness settles again on the slope of Busarchili.

It's snowing.

Twelve-year-old Gigia Bubunauri is going up along the slope of Kvenamta Mountain. A gun which belonged to his father is slung over his shoulder.

The shrine of the Village Angel[4] is at the top of the hill. Gigia is going in another direction. Suddenly he stops. He looks around. Then he continues his journey. Then he stops again and decides to turn back. Somehow, his heart is drawing

---

4 *Adgilis Deda*: literally, 'Place Mother', a pagan protective spirit associated with a given place.

him to the shrine. But he still goes in another direction.

Suddenly his foot slipped and he fell. Standing up, he brushed off the rustling snow. He turned back and went along the slope up to the shrine.

From the ridge of the hill, Gigia saw the eagle and quickened his pace upwards.

He really wanted to see the eagle up close. He crouched down and went up stealthily.

The eagle's cry disturbed the calm of the snow. Then it flapped its wings violently against the hill, kicking up a blizzard around itself. It cried out again forcefully and went quiet.

Gigia didn't dare get close to the eagle; he kept an eye on it from far away. Somehow watching the eagle always gave him a particular kind of pleasure. But he had never seen it up close.

The eagle kicked up a blizzard around itself on the hill again. Then it went up into the air and Gigia saw that it had something hanging from its foot. He dropped his gun and moved closer.

The eagle cried out and rushed towards the boy with a whoosh.

Gigia stood and watched.

Human footprints left in yesterday's snow were half-filled by fresh snow. The chain of a metal trap was attached to the shrine. The eagle's right claw was caught in the trap. Gigia was examining the footprints. Then he watched the eagle for a long time. There were silver coins scattered inside the shrine. Small bells were hanging from sun-bleached deer antlers. It was snowing and the gentle tinkling of the bells was joining the rustling of the snow. The soot-blackened remains of candles on the stones of the shrine made the whole place calmer and more mysterious. Everything was like the blessings of the sky: the shrine, the snow, the pale deer antlers and the tinkling of the bells, mingling with the rustling of the snow, which was unravelling the harmony of nature; the metal trap attached to the chain, the eagle caught in the trap and beyond that, the strange footprints lingering in the old snow, which were gradually being filled up by the fresh snow.

Gigia Bubunauri went up to the eagle. It cried again, and panting, rushed at the boy. Then it stood suddenly, closed its wings and stared at Gigia. Gigia released its foot from the trap. Blood came gushing out of the eagle. One claw was just barely hanging on by the skin.

Gigia Bubunauri brought the eagle home.

It's still snowing...

The soot-blackened towers stand like exclamation marks in the snow. Smoke comes up here and there and sways slowly, the clotted smoke blending sluggishly with the snowy stillness.

The scene inside the Bubunauri tower: a fire is burning in the hearth. The ceiling is blackened with soot, and from the darkness, the oak beams holding up the roof look out at the whiteness of the snow. Military equipment is hanging on the wall: a shield, a sword, a gauntlet, a chain, a helmet, daggers, a gun and even a soot-blackened bow and arrows, an old witness to the life of the Bubunauri name, beset by enemies.

From the rafters, the shrivelled and blackened right hands of several men were hanging.[5] Further up, in a corner where the light of the fire couldn't reach, a huge pair of ibex horns hung from a chain.

It's snowing outside.

---

5 The right hands of blood enemies were cut off and collected for centuries.

HUMAN SADNESS

Pale light comes in from the roof.

Twelve-year-old Gigia Bubunauri and the eagle were sitting on an ibex skin spread on the floor.

The eagle was looking around at the walls of the house with a calm gaze.

Gigia stood up and took a silver dagger from the wall. He took a silver chalice from a chest and brought strong vodka in a silver pitcher. Then he poured vodka into the chalice and scraped some silver from the pitcher with the edge of the dagger. He dropped the silver scrapings into the cup, stirred and set it on the floor in front of him.

The eagle was calmly watching Gigia, who, like a mature man, gradually lifted his head, looked at the eagle and said: "I am Gigia Bubunauri, son of Badzia, the last descendant of the Bubunauri name. I have a mother, and a sister who is married and lives on the other side of the village, who has three children: Nino, Shorena and Gagi. All three of them are small; Gagi doesn't even know how to walk yet.

"I have a blood enemy. Like I just told you, I am the only one left to carry on the Bubunauri name. Most of my ancestors were killed by their enemies. My father was killed by Khevsurians from the other side of the mountains, too. It was winter, they couldn't carry the dead body in the deep snow, so they brought it back in pieces in their saddlebags; I was five years old then. The Tagvauris are my blood enemies. I always try to avoid going up that mountain. Don't think that I'm afraid of my blood enemies. Even now, I could carry on the blood feud, but I would be ashamed, I would be ashamed for my ancestors. I don't want to senselessly cut off our family name. First, I must marry and father an heir, then I will be ready for the blood feud, and if they kill me, it's nothing. There will be someone left to carry on the name. By the way, I don't want to kill anyone, but there's something in my blood that shouts: 'Don't dishonour the name, child!' I know it's the voice of my ancestors, but I'm still waiting. First, I'll continue the name and then…"

Gigia went quiet, and in an even quieter voice said: "I was betrothed to Mzia Tamniauri from the cradle. There, you see that village on the other side, that's where she lives. She's only eight. She has hair the colour of the sun. On the village saint's day I've seen her many times from a distance. My father was still alive when they engaged us.

"Yes, I always try to avoid going up that mountain. I don't even like to look at it. Don't think that I don't like heights, actually I like them. I also like Mzia. You probably understand love completely differently. You're always in the sky and you can dream better than me.

"In my opinion, love is the dream of eternal life. So that's why I don't want to die yet. First, I must carry on the name. God created love so that we would carry on our names. The love of a woman is the beginning of that great love, which is called eternal life. I must continue this love first. You may understand it differently, but we on earth probably dream much less than you in the sky. If only you knew how I want to fly in the sky sometimes! How lucky you are—you can be on the earth and in the sky, too.

"You're terribly brave.

"I want to be like you, too, but it won't happen, God made me to stay on the earth. That's why I told you everything, because I want you to know my story. You're brave and you should understand. You must swear to be my brother. Even though I can't fly in the sky, when I see you up there, at least I can say, that's my brother."

Gigia went quiet. Then he looked the eagle in the eyes. The eagle was listening calmly.

Gigia Bubunauri cut his right hand with the edge of the dagger, then he lifted the eagle's bloody foot and mixed its blood with his blood, and he took the chalice with vodka and silver scrapings and said to the eagle:

"Your mother, my mother!

Your sister, my sister!

Your brother, my brother!

Your joy, my joy!

Your worry, my worry!

If anyone upsets you, they upset me!

Someone kills you, they kill me!

Your life, my life!

Your oath, eternally!

Our brotherhood, forever!

Amen!" he said finally and took a sip of vodka from the chalice. Then he made the eagle take a gulp. He bathed the wound in the remaining vodka, bandaged it, brought the eagle outside and released it.

It was snowing.

For a long time, the eagle circled around high above the Bubunauri tower.

It was snowing.

Then gradually, darkness fell.

The eagle cried out several times and flew away towards the rocky mountains.

HUMAN SADNESS

That spring Gigia Bubunauri turned thirteen.

The violet-patterned spring was calling Gigia and his peers to the high mountains.

Only Gigia had a gun. The boys hurried along up to the ridge of the hill. When they reached the peak, they rested.

The sun was rising over the Saqorne Mountains.

The boys lay back and watched the sky. Somewhere an eagle cried. Then some ravens started cawing.

Above the boys' heads, the eagle drew circles in the sky and slowly moved downward. Suddenly one of Gigia's friends grabbed the gun. Gigia immediately came to his senses and instinctively clutched at the gun. The boy pulled the trigger.

"It's an eagle, man!"

"Don't shoot!" Gigia just managed to say this, then suddenly a shot rang out; first Gigia jumped up high, then he fell face-down in the sunlit grass.

The boys stood in silence, even the one who had accidentally fired the shot. Suddenly he turned around and ran down towards the village, wailing.

The men covered a stretcher with new spring leaves and laid Gigia Bubunauri down as gently as that winter's snowflakes had lain on the village shrine's soot-blackened stones.

Gigia's mother wasn't at home. That day, Gigia's niece, little Gagi, took her first steps, when she was away for a visit.

They laid Gigia by the hearth, right where he had sworn brotherhood with the eagle. Some men ran to fetch the doctor, but it was too late; nor was his mother able to see how, by the hearth in the family's tower, the last Bubunauri descendant ended the ancient and beleaguered family name. That day, the voice that shouted, "Don't dishonour the name, child!" the

HUMAN SADNESS

Bubunauri blood finally fell silent forever. All that remained was the tower, the soot-blackened roof, and hanging on the wall, a sword, a shield, a gauntlet, a chain, a helmet, a soot-blackened bow and arrows. Hanging from the rafters, the shrivelled and blackened right hands of several men, these old witnesses to the life of the Bubunauri name, beset by enemies. There also remained the mountains, the Village Angel shrine, Gigia's village, the graveyard above the village, the stony grave flooded with tears, knelt over by mourners in black, and one more: Gigia Bubunauri's eagle blood brother, who perched on Gigia's grave on the third day and never flew away.

At first the village dogs decided to go after the eagle, but they found themselves in such trouble that they ran back towards the village with their tails between their legs.

The eagle sat still and didn't fly away. One day, the boy who had pulled the trigger decided to get revenge and ambushed it with a cudgel, since the eagle was the reason he fired. He approached and started beating it with the cudgel. At first the eagle was patient, then it trapped the boy in its claws and pecked out both of his eyes.

They swarmed out of the village and shot the eagle.

For a short time it lay on the ground, then it got upright again, but the men trapped it underfoot and started kicking it to death. It straightened up again, propped its wings up on the ground, rolled its eyes terribly at the people, opened its mouth, gasped and spat blood at them.

Then it dug its claws deeply into the earth of Gigia's grave and died on the spot.

The men went down silently towards the village. A little

girl of eight or nine years old, dressed in black, was coming up from below so quietly that it was as if she was afraid of everything surrounding her…

At the end, there is a note from the author:

"Eh, Mother Earth! Your heart would break if you knew how melancholy it makes me to see a Georgian woman dressed in black on your shoulders!"

WORRY NO. 1682

"Name and surname."

"Martia Bubunauri."

"What's worrying you?"

"Loneliness worries me. You can spend time among people, but even so you feel lonely. Sometimes you feel like a stranger to yourself and run away from yourself. Why does this happen? I don't know. Where do we come from and where do we go? I also don't know."

THE SOUL

"Name and surname."

"Martia Bubunauri."

"What is the soul like?"

"The soul is like a scythe that rusts easily. Your past is like rust. Every now and then you need to scrape it off, like how you scrape a dagger with a whetstone. The flesh gets rusty as well from time to time, it corrodes and blunts the soul. That's how it is. When you get old the soul and the body are pulled towards the earth, the earth is calling, and then the soul gets softer."

THE FIRST DISAPPOINTMENT
(from the *Chronicles* notebook)

The priest was very disappointed that there were no walnut trees in Busarchili, but he still gave a friendly speech in parting.

We are now heading towards Salagho. There are bad rumours about that village and caution is needed. Most of the people in the village are supposed to be mad and we might not even be able to enter it.

The Commander-in-Chief laid siege to Salagho. They didn't even notice us.

"We need to be civilised with the madmen," the Commander-in-Chief said and we entered the village.

In the very middle of the village, the madmen have tied a person to a tree and are pricking him with knives. The man is bruised, but he is not dying yet. Someone is begging the madmen to leave him alone, but they carried on.

"Fire your guns!" the Commander-in-Chief ordered.

The guns roared and the madmen froze in place when they heard this sound.

"Why are you torturing this man?" the commander asked.

HUMAN SADNESS

"He isn't telling—that's why."
"What is he meant to tell you?"
"What he has seen in the beyond."

A STRANGE TALE
(a little story from the *Human Sadness* notebook)

One year ago, Bagila Aldiauri woke up and when he got up, he saw the shape of his soul coming out from his body like a shadow. The soul carried the body outside and looked around. The Salagho villagers were just getting up and getting ready for work.

"Come here, all of you!" the shadow shouted at the people.

They gathered by Bagila's door and when they saw the body and the shadow separated, they shivered on the spot.

"You see my body? I will take it inside the house; I will prop it up in the attic and go to the next world. Until I come back, don't lay a hand on it, don't bury it, or you'll be in trouble."

The shadow thrust the body under his arm and leant it in the corner right above the door. He came out and left…

That day, twelve people went mad in Salagho. One year later, the soul came back again, once again like a shadow; he went inside the house and carried his body out, all shrivelled and worm-eaten, then he shook it out in the sun and took it back inside. Suddenly the body came back to life and became a man again. That day, more than half of the village went mad. They tied him to a pole and carried him, torturing him with questions: "Tell us what was there and why you aren't dead." He doesn't tell them that he has a small snake in his body. It goes around and around, this snake, and licks his wounds. The snake doesn't want to kill Bagila; it only licks and licks. Apparently, the snake was given to him in the other world and he was told: "Take it. Put this snake in your body, and whatever happens, it won't kill you. In fact, it will cure you. If you get tired of being human and your heart longs to be here, rip the snake's tail off; then it will lose its power, you will die and come back here."

The madmen were beating him, poking him with daggers, but Bagila wouldn't rip the snake's tail off. He didn't want to go back there.

The madmen couldn't catch the snake. Only Bagila could catch it.

They were torturing him and he didn't make a sound.

That's the way things are.

EVASION
(from the *Chronicles* notebook)

We couldn't understand the madmen. Neither do they have our philosophy, nor do any walnut trees grow there. We preferred to avoid them.

We headed toward Atnokhi and we had soon unfurled our banner up on the upper rooftops in the rays of the sun. They swore wordless obedience to us. They're all women; there's only one man. We will first and foremost begin questioning this man.

THE RIGHT HAND
(from *The Author's Notebook*)

Ghenja from Bosili chose Goria from Atnokhi as his best man. He took a woman from Khviralaanti as his wife. Ghenja had an arrangement with the Kists to work for them as a shepherd and he left a month after the wedding. He left the woman in the cattle shed.

The road from Bosili to Atnokhi goes through the forest. It's autumn. Ghenja's wife had gathered some twigs and is preparing them in bundles to carry back.

Goria from Atnokhi passed along on the road, grabbed his friend's wife[6] and disappeared with her into the forest.

A man passed and noticed the bundle of twigs. The man continued on his way. Some time later, Ghenja's wife continued on her way, loaded up with the twigs.

Five years later, Ghenja brought his wife with him to where he worked with the Kists. It was the same there as it had been before; he rarely came home.

"Why don't you stay at home? I was bothered back there and it seems it will be the same here…"

"What?" asked Ghenja, "Who bothered you?"

"No, no one, but…"

"Come with me up the mountain and bring the child, too," said Ghenja.

---

6 *natlideda*: the mother of one's godchild. Usually the groom's best man would become the godfather of the couple's children.

HUMAN SADNESS

The woman and child followed him.

When they reached the top of the mountain, he wrestled the woman to the ground and pressed a dagger to her throat.

"Now will you tell me, whose child is this?"

The woman had no choice; she told him everything.

"Since he didn't look like me, I knew right away that he wasn't mine," said Ghenja and...

The woman came down the hill sobbing, carrying the child's head in her skirts.

Ghenja went to Atnokhi and asked for Goria.

"He's up on the mountain, with the flock," said Goria's wife.

"Are you well?" asked Ghenja.

"Yes, may God bless you, too. Come inside, it's as if you've forgotten us."

"I'll go up. I'll find Goria and we'll come back together," said Ghenja, and he went up the mountain.

Goria was sitting among the birch trees. He and Ghenja asked after each other sincerely. Ghenja was holding a small axe.

"What are you doing with that axe?" Goria was surprised.

"This winter we're going to move nearby, and I want to cut some birch to make a broom."[7]

They carried on talking.

"Well, goodbye," said Ghenja and shook his hand. He held the axe in his left hand. When he shook Goria's hand, he didn't let go. He pressed it against a birch tree, swung the axe and cut it off.

---

7 Customarily, making a broom was one of the first steps in preparing to build a new house.

"Goodbye," said Ghenja, and he pulled Goria's trousers down and left.

In the evening Goria appeared in the village, trousers round his ankles, carrying his severed right hand in his left hand; somehow he had managed to wrap his shirt around his wounded arm.

Even now he keeps his severed hand. Now and then he airs it out in the sun, because he keeps it in a chest.

WORRY NO. 1683

"Goria Aptsiauri."

"What's worrying you?"

"Women don't like me because I only have one hand."

GORIA

(from *The Notebook of the World*)

"What do you love most of all?"

"Hahaha! Why, women of course!"

"Do you love life?"

"Me?"

"Yes."

"I suppose I love life as long as God keeps me alive. God breathes life into everyone, but only good people stand beside Him."

"What is life?"

"Life is a god. Both this world and the next one belong to him. Life and death are different gods and together they form the Lord."

"What holds up the Earth?"

"It holds it up."

"What do you mean by *it*?"

"Love."

"If they told you to go to the moon, would you go?"

"If they let me take a pretty woman with me, then I would go."

"Your time for women has been and gone. You got old; take your wife."

"I am sick to death of her. What would I need her for?"

"Have you ever had any nice dreams?"

"I have, but the devil can take it. Sometimes there were women, but then I'd wake up, and where were they?"

"What world are dreams in?"

"I can't tell you, but even when the bones are scattered in the ground, the soul still exists. I think the soul and dreams belong to the same world."

"You'll go to the next world, won't you?"

"Everyone will go there and I will too."

"If they sent you back after a while to this world, would you come back?"

"Yes, I would. Why wouldn't I?"

"You wouldn't know anyone here?"

"Come on, what's the big deal about getting to know people? Within an hour or two I'll have met a woman and..."

"Hold on a second, I'm asking you philosophical questions

and you're still talking about women."

"…what could be more philosophical than women?"

"Apart from women, what else do you wish for?"

"I saw the violets on the graves that spring up from between the bones. When the owner of the bones was alive, he must have wanted something, but not that. But I want it."

THE TRIUMPHAL CAMPAIGN
(from the *Chronicles* notebook)

Midday. The priest finished inspecting the Atnokhians' walnut trees and gave a long speech afterwards.

The Commander-in-Chief assembled the troops.

We are expecting a great holiday today. The whole of Gudamaqari is in our hands when it comes to walnut trees and women. Only one village is left: Didebani. This is the village that has disobeyed us; therefore, we have saved it for last and this manœuvre is the cleverest of all. Now that all the villages have unanimously sworn an oath to us on the clan icon, Didebani has no choice any more. Unless they welcome us obediently… who knows if they thought we might invade them first? They were wrong, sorely wrong, and waiting has shattered their resolve.

Our troops set out for Didebani. The spies were intending to go there, but the Commander-in-Chief changed his mind.

"Spies, there's no need for you to go there any more. Go to our village and inform them that we are entering Didebani in triumph today and we will bring Ketino back to Chokhi this evening. Tell them to make preparations for the wedding. I feel in my heart that they will welcome us right there on the road and surrender the woman to us. Go to one of your naval divisions and tell them to send a fish from the fish-farm for the wedding and to select some trout. Let's take our captive with us and give him something good to eat. What can be done? He is our enemy, but we are the victors.

"Shete! Cheer up, lad! Tonight we will seat Ketino next to you at table."

"Now! To the right!" he ordered to the army.

"Forward, march, on the double!" he ordered and we set out for Didebani singing and with the bells ringing. We have our own battle anthem that was composed by none other than our writer. This song goes like this:

> *Is there anything that isn't ours,*
> *From one end to another*
> *er-er-er-er-er-er-er!*

The *errrr!* at the end is meant to go on for a long time.

The midday sun is blazing in the clear sky. We do not stop singing. The bellringer rings the bells. Only four kilometres lie between us and our goal.

Oh, how glorious this moment is! Look, Didebani has already come into view.

"Sing louder and let us march into the village!" the Commander-in-Chief ordered.

The troops roared. Shete was glowing.

"This evening I will have a wife," he said.

The bells are ringing. We moved ahead.

Now the people have appeared.

The Commander-in-Chief's premonition that the people would come out of the village came true. It turns out that they are coming out to meet us, carrying something slowly, perhaps a gift.

"Raise your voices!" the Commander-in-Chief ordered.

We are going towards the people, singing.

They stopped in their tracks.

What happened? They are weeping, weeping out loud!

"They are weeping for joy; they are glad that they will swear an oath of obedience to such a renowned people as us. Or, perhaps they are weeping because their conscience is tormented," the priest explained to us.

"Sing!" Vazhi Gogi shouted.

"Our singing is suppressing their weeping."

Oh, what a glorious moment it is! Some are singing, others are weeping and soon our singing will suppress their weeping.

Just three steps and...

What is happening?

"Halt!" the Commander-in-Chief ordered us.

A coffin? Ah, this must be why they were weeping.

KETINO
(a real story from the *Human Sadness* notebook)

Ketino and Mikho went to school together until year six. Then Mikho went to Pasanauri to continue studying. In Kitokhi, where they had studied together, there were only six classes, so Ketino's parents stopped her going to school.

Their villages are side by side. Mikho is from Kitokhi; Ketino is from Didebani.

From childhood, they were always together and couldn't stand being apart from each other. At first, when Mikho moved away, he would rush back to Gudamaqari every two or three days to see Ketino.

"And then?"

"Then, as they say, out of sight, out of mind. Mikho became cold-hearted and came back only occasionally. In the end he went off to university and hasn't been back in a year."

Ketino fell more in love with Mikho than ever before, and one day she went to the city to see him.

"Did she know his address?"

"No, she went, saying, 'Perhaps I'll run into him.' In fact, she did run into him in the street. Mikho was taken aback: he realised he loved her but for some reason he still acted cold-hearted."

"Come on, let's go to the cinema," said Ketino.

They went. They joined the queue. Mikho dug around in his pockets and found just enough money for two tickets. "Good, I didn't embarrass myself," he thought in his heart. Ketino noticed this, but pretended she hadn't.

"Mikho, are you buying the tickets?" some girls shouted from behind, "Get three for us!"

Mikho shrugged.

Without letting the girls see, Ketino put a five-rouble note in Mikho's hand.

HUMAN SADNESS

When the film was over, Mikho didn't make a sound. He walked Ketino to the bus station without saying a word to her. Then suddenly he exploded and nearly shouted at her: "Why are you following me? Why did you come here?"

Ketino was lost for words.

Then the bus took her back to Gudamaqari.

Ten days later, she received a letter. She knew from the handwriting that it was from Mikho. Shivering, she opened it and five roubles fell into her hand.

Late at night, when her parents had gone to sleep, she hung a rope from the rafters…

The village wouldn't let Ketino's grave be dug with all the others, saying, "She's a self-killer."

Our triumphal campaign came to an end at her grave.

Just as we were burying her, Galilei rushed over and from a distance shouted at us: "Where have you been? The wedding feast is already prepared!" When he came closer and saw our pallid faces, he asked: "Where is Ketino?"

"This is her, the one they're throwing dirt on," Shete indicated.

"What are you doing? Damn you! Who are you throwing dirt on?" roared Galilei and he raged at us, throwing whatever he could get his hands on.

Then several men dragged him away forcefully.

"I'll knock your blocks off!" he shouted on the way.

Ketino's grave remained a black mark in Gudamaqari, blanketed with snow.

Soundlessly, we turned back; mutely, we reached Chokhi.

That evening we released the prisoner. The Commander-in-Chief sent the spies to discharge the naval division.

HUMAN SADNESS

After all this, spring did not delay for long. The shepherds drove their flocks back from the winter pastures and Gudamaqari Gorge was filled with sound. The people who wintered down in the valley came back up for the summer, too.

FROM THE AUTHOR

These writings were kept for us by our grandmother who we buried the year before last. The 'Gudamaqari Warriors' are for the most part still alive today. As for Gamikhardai, he was probably following them up a mountain loaded with his backpack. In his bag were the worries of the Gudamaqari villagers and he would spend the night up some mountain or other. He said gods love heights and maybe one of them might be there on a mountain top.

The shepherds took pity on him. One of them got dressed up completely in white, stuck a beard of wool on to make him look like God and they put him on a mountain top for Gamikhardai.

Gamikhardai saw the shepherd in white from afar and came straightaway to this God on his knees.

"Glory to you, O Lord!" he said as he came.

"What's the matter?" God asked.

"Oh God, I have this bag full of the Gudamaqari villagers' worries. Please dispel them, give your blessing," Gamikhardai took the bag off his shoulders.

"Oh!" the shepherd sighed. "There's a lot of them. Let's agree on one thing: pick one of the worries, the one that is deepest in your heart, for me to dispel and I shall dispel it. Ask for no more."

Then Gamikhardai took this worry from the bag:

WORRY NO. 1

"Name and first name."
"Giorgi Bekauri."
"What's worrying you?"

> *War is about to break,*
> *The troops hear the call.*
> *The Earth will shake,*
> *The moon will fall."*

God read this worry, then touched Gamikhardai's shoulder and said: "I will resolve this worry for you."

Gamikhardai took the rest of the worries away and he was happy. As long as God resolves this worry, to hell with our remaining worries. They can stay with us.

In the campaign writer's notebook, on which is written *Human Sadness*, is one story that has nothing to do with the campaign. It must have been written later. I liked this story and I present it below with no changes.

CAROUSING WITH DEATH
(a story from the *Human Sadness* notebook)

In Gudamaqari Gorge, to the east of Chokhi village, there is a mountain the locals call Elijah's Mountain.

In the view of the people, the dwelling-place of God is on the mountain top and they have built shrines on it. A boundary stone has been placed midway up the mountainside. Above the stone is God's dwelling-place and below it is the place of the demons, concealed deep in the gorge.

Each year, a kid is slaughtered at the shrine and the priest's helpers cast the headless body of the kid down from the top of the mountain. The people, standing above the boundary stone, try to catch the kid as it comes rolling down the mountain, and if they succeed, they cook it and everybody gets his own piece of meat to eat.

If it passes the boundary stone, it is called the 'Devil's Piece' and they give up and go home disappointed.

Daybreak. The first ray of sunlight fell on Gudamaqari Gorge and the mist stretching out along the bank of the Aragvi was rent in twain; one half went up the slope of Elijah's Mountain and the other half remained in the gorge, fell across the Aragvi like a blanket, thinned out and sank down into the river.

The sun lit up Gudamaqari Gorge.

Early in the morning, the people began to congregate in the chapel of St George in Chokhi. Up came Bibghai, the scrawny priest with the crooked jaw. Then came Omara's Sandruai and Shughlia's Zorai and they were followed by Korai, Gamikhardai, Shete, Basai, Mtsariai, Chichqai, Jghunai and Tatiai, and eventually the Chokhians started to arrive in a continuous stream. They would walk up the hill, kneel down, make the sign of the cross, prostrate themselves three times and afterwards sit in the gathering place around the shrine. The women, meanwhile, would stop below the shrine, by the boundary stone; they would pray there and then join the other women. According to the rules of the clan, it was forbidden for women to set foot on the mountain where the shrine was. Only the men could walk on it and then only on saints' days: on ordinary days they, too, avoided profaning the grounds of the shrine.

A monk came up, said a prayer, prostrated himself three times and went over to the people.

"May the mercy of the shrine be with all of you," the monk said.

"And with you," the people answered.

Jghunai handed a drinking bowl with beer to the monk. The monk took it, said a prayer and drank it.

"Monk, you know that this year you have to offer up the kid—it's your turn," Bibghai said.

"I know," the monk answered, "I've sent a child up the mountain to get one."

"Let's not waste any time," Bibghai said and stood up. Everybody was staring at him. This old man had such a pleasant appearance that the people could barely take their eyes off him. He was tall and lanky; only his jaw was crooked and this only accentuated his austere mien.

HUMAN SADNESS

A little boy came into view above the village. He was carrying a white kid on his shoulders. He came up and stood next to the monk. The kid licked the weary boy's hair and then glanced around at the people and bleated.

"Let's collect the candles and not lose any time!" the priest said to his helpers.

The helpers went around the people and took three candles from each.

"Mercy to the monk!"

"Mercy to Jghunai!"

"Mercy to Martiai!"

"Mercy to Korai!" the helpers were shouting as they gathered the candles.

"Come on, let's go!" Bibghai said and draped the banner decorated with small bells across his shoulders and led the people towards Elijah's Mountain. Only the women remained where they were. They stood on their feet and watched the people going up the mountainside. A boy about twelve years of age was leading with the kid on his shoulders, the priest walking behind him jingling the bells, and the priest's helpers and the other Chokhians following at a distance.

The priest ordered the boy to go ahead and to bring the kid up to the mountain top. The boy went quickly. The priest lined the people up above the boundary stone and began to follow the slope up toward the mountain top.

The boy was waiting by the shrine for the priest to come. He was holding the kid by the front feet and cuddling it. The small goat was snow-white with sky-blue eyes. It was licking the boy's cheek with its tongue and bleating as though it were speaking to him.

HUMAN SADNESS

The priest was gradually approaching. Countless goat-heads lay next to the boundary stone at the summit of Elijah's Mountain. Some of them had already been pulverised with the passing of time. Some though, had retained the shape of a head. It was a rule that the heads were left there after they had been cut off and it turned out that the wild animals avoided going up there because the mountain was so tall; only the crows and ravens would sit there from time to time, eat the carrion and then leave the bones behind. It was for this reason that the bones had piled up there over time, so many of them that if the Creator desired to breathe life back into the goat-heads and these heads all bleated up towards heaven, heaven would be rent with pity. Today, another head was to be added to these gnarled bones.

The priest went up onto the mountain, knelt down and prostrated himself three times. Then he came over and lit the candles that his helpers had collected, and prayed for a long time. He was beseeching Elijah to preserve the Chokhians by his power, that they might escape hailstones and the tempest, that avalanches might keep far away from them and that no flood might come...

The boy was standing there, holding the goat in one hand, leaning forward and listening.

Bibghai finished saying the prayer, stuck the candles on the blackened stones of the shrine and took out a dagger. The boy turned the kid upside-down, held its feet in both of his hands and afterwards, when the priest had tipped the kid's head back in order to slit its throat, the boy looked to the side. Now all he could see was the top of the mountain opposite and all he could feel in his whole body was the priest cutting off the kid's head. After that, the boy let go of the headless, twitching body of the goat.

The priest pinned the head of the goat to the shrine; then he took the headless body of the goat, threw it down towards the people and cried out: "Long live Elijah and Zachariah!"

"Long may they live!" the people cried out from below and rushed up to catch the goat, lest it miss the boundary stone such that they would not be able to eat it. As it happened, they caught it quickly and waited there for the priest.

"Let's go," Bibghai said to the boy, who was staring at the head of the kid pinned to the shrine. The head was blinking its eyes.

"Let's go. What are you staring at?" Bibghai said again.

"It's not dying," the boy said.

"It will die. What else could happen?" Bibghai said, putting the banner on his shoulder, and went down the hill. The boy followed after him, then stopped and listened intently.

"Did you hear?" the boy asked.

"What?"

"The kid just bleated."

"You probably imagined it," the priest said, but at that very moment the goat's voice rang out. They turned around and stared, stunned, at the severed head.

Blood was dripping from the head, drop by drop. It was staring back at the boy and the priest with equally stunned eyes, which were blinking every so often, and its tongue, dry from the lack of water, was flicking back and forth in the air. The candles that were gathered on the stones were sputtering and the drops of blood were falling down onto them and sizzling. The bones scattered all around were spattered with blood. The kid's head was staring at both the boy and the priest.

"Why is it not dying?" the boy asked.

"Sometimes it happens that it takes time for death to come calling," the priest replied.

"Will death not come?"

"That is not possible…"

"Why?"

"That's the rule."

"What rule?"

"The rule of life and death," the priest explained, making the sign of the cross and turning around. The boy took one more look at the kid's head, which was flicking its desiccated tongue back and forth in the air, and followed the priest. There was fear in his eyes.

When they came to the people, they were struck with fear: the body of the kid was thrashing about.

"It's not dying," the monk said.

The priest did not make a sound, led the people on ahead and went up to the hill with the shrine.

The people waited for a long time for the kid to die, but it kept thrashing until it did not have a single drop of blood left in its veins and then it quieted down until it was only barely thumping.

"It's dead," the monk said and skinned it.

The people mustered at the village gathering place and started drinking, and the monk put the meat from the kid on the fire. Jghunai brought beer to the women. They were playing the accordion and the pleasant rumbling of music filled the entire area around the hilltop shrine. The Chokhians grew merry. The dancing picked up.

HUMAN SADNESS

Suddenly, the music stopped; the girl with the accordion was the first to see a remarkable-looking young man walking towards them. Everyone looked in that direction and a silence fell as if they had all gone mute.

The young man walked towards the hilltop shrine; he was dressed in a light raiment in the colour of a spring butterfly and his blonde curls were resting upon his shoulders; he came and knelt on the hill, prostrated himself three times, stood up, went over to the people and said: "The mercy of the shrine be upon you!"

"And upon you, too!" they bumbled back at the stranger, captivated by his beauty.

"May I join you?" the newcomer asked and when he smiled, his face shone with such kindness that a smile spread across the face of everyone around him.

"Yes, you may, why not? The guest is from God," they said boldly and invited him to sit at the head of the table.

"Over here, over here!"

They brought him over and seated him next to the priest. Jghunai served him some beer in a drinking bowl. He took the bowl and pronounced a toast: "Cheers, people of Chokhi! Be well and may God grant you kindness and love!"

"And to you as well!" they shouted from all around. He tipped the bowl up against his lips with great relish and when he finished, he smiled.

"While we're bringing out the meat, have some bread," the priest said, handing him a ritual pastry.

"Thank you," the stranger said courteously. The people were taken aback by this courtesy. Then the monk brought the cooked meat on a platter and set it down on the banquet table.

HUMAN SADNESS

The meat was steaming hot.

"Come on, guest, drink one to our health!" Jghunai said, handing him a horn with raki… he took it, made a toast and passed the horn back.

"Drink!" Jghunai said.

"I'm not used to it. I won't drink any."

"What? Are you not a man? How come you won't drink just one horn full, as a toast to our meeting, and to you, latecomer?"

The guest tipped the horn to his lips, and from the expression on his face, it was evident that he found it hard to drink.

"Take some meat," the monk said.

"No, I don't eat meat," he refused and reached for another pastry.

The people who were there were surprised by this proclamation. They were eating the meat from the kid so heartily that they couldn't understand why the guest would refuse such a pleasure.

The eating and drinking began in earnest. The Chokhians were draining horn after horn and the raki and beer eventually had their way with them. They also tried to make the guest drink, but he refused.

The women at the bottom of the hill came to like the guest so much that they forgot that they needed to stay below the boundary stone. They came up closer in order to peer at the beauty of the new arrival. The priest noticed this; he got up, rang the bell and thereby gave a sign to the women that they had to go back down. With a quiet whisper, they moved down past the boundary stone and started dancing.

HUMAN SADNESS

The men were already quite drunk. They were singing. Now they compelled the guest even more strongly to drink the raki, but he wouldn't drink any more; he only made a toast and handed the horn back to Jghunai.

"I don't like your attitude!" Jghunai said and bristled quarrelsomely.

"Jghunai!" the monk shouted at him.

"What do you want?"

"You are wrong, Jghunai!" the monk said and stood in between the guest and Jghunai.

"I said what I said and I'll say it again: if you take the horn, you have to drink from it," Jghunai shouted.

The women were dancing down below.

"Come down! Come down!" they shouted up at the youngsters.

"Don't get upset. Jghunai insists like this with everyone," the monk said to the guest.

"I'm not. Why should I be upset?" the guest said.

In the meantime, the time had come when, according to their custom, the Chokhians would test each other's strength. In front of the shrine, on a flat expanse, they set down a cask full of beer and the young people stood around it.

Some of them grabbed the cask with their hands.

"What are they going to do?" the guest asked.

"They are testing their strength; whoever is strong enough will push the cask over."

"Could I also try?"

"Yes, you can. Go on," the monk said and brought the guest over to the cask. This turn of events set the hearts of the curious Chokhians racing and they stood all around the young people who were encircling the cask, who were all trying, on their part, to push the cask over. They didn't have to wait long: the guest gave the cask such a mighty shove that he took the youngsters with him.

The women started whispering among themselves. Jghunai also bristled quarrelsomely, but they calmed him down and they passed around a drink as a toast to the brave young guest. According to their rule, the beer which was in this cask was to be drunk as a toast to the victor.[8]

Then the priest took a drinking bowl, and before he began the prayer, he said modestly: "Guest, please don't get upset with us if we ask you your name, but we have a rule that your name has to be said in the toast…"

"Death," the guest replied.

"What?!"

"My name is Death."

The people suddenly fell completely quiet. The priest nearly dropped the bowl he was holding.

"Really?!"

"Yes, really," Death said and he smiled, too. The people also smiled when they saw his face.

"He's lying," somebody guffawed.

"No, no, I'm not lying. I am Death."

"Then what do you want here?"

"What do you mean by 'what do I want'? If I hadn't wanted to, I wouldn't have come."

"Come on, don't drive us mad, tell us, who are you?"

---

8 *kargi qma*: literally, 'brave man' or 'good man'; there was a custom that a toast was to be drunk to whoever pushed the barrel over, who was called *kargi qma*.

"I am Death. I missed being human with you all and that's why I came. I can be human for one day in a million years, and today is the day."

"Begone, devil! Begone, devil!" the people squawked.

"Wait, listen to me, aren't you interested?" said Death. The people fell silent.

"My time as a human being will end at sundown today. Then I will turn into Death again. Do you know why I came? I really missed you."

"We know, we know!" said Jghunai.

"Jghunai, no matter how angry you get, I won't get into it with you, I have only one day to be human, and what's the point of fighting with you?"

"Don't lie!" Jghunai got angry.

"What am I lying about...?"

"You're not Death, you're just Kirakozai,[9] a good-for-nothing, whoever you are."

"Why don't you believe it? It doesn't matter. If you want, don't believe it. That will make me even happier. Today is the day when not a single soul on earth will die."

"What about this kid?" asked Jghunai and he waved a gnawed-up bone before Death's eyes.

"It hasn't died."

"How? Didn't we eat it just now? Didn't you see? Didn't you say that you don't eat meat?"

"Yes, I said that..."

"So?!"

"So, that kid didn't die, either."

"What rubbish this man is talking!"

9 *Kirakozai*: a given name associated with liars.

"It was impossible for it to die because today God turned me into a human and I will be one until the sun goes down. I alone can be killed, nobody and nothing else. This kid is still alive and right now the head is coming to rejoin the bones…"

The people looked over there. The head rolled over the hills, stopped at the boundary stone and stared at the people; it wagged its dry tongue and bleated. That very moment, it rolled over and left with all the bones which belonged to it. Its skin, which had been hung on a tree, followed along, too…

The people trembled with fear and couldn't make a sound.

"What are you scared of, people? I came to have a good time with you, but you… let's sit, let's drink to my victory." The people assented and handed round the drinking bowl.

"Cheers to Death!" said the priest.

"Cheers! Cheers! Long live living Death!"

Death grew merry: he emptied one horn after another and sang. The people grew accustomed to him again. The monk fell in love with him so much that he wouldn't leave his side, then they swore an oath of brotherhood: they scraped silver into a bowl of raki and drank it.

"From now on, if anyone upsets you, they upset me," said the monk to Death, and glanced at Jghunai.

Down below, the women were still dancing. Death stood up and went down to dance. None of the women would give one another the chance to dance with him.

A black-clad woman arrived from Didebani. Leaning on a stick, she looked at Death with a piercing gaze and asked: "Why did you kill my Ketino?"

"Mother, I have one day to be a human, I beg you, please don't ruin it!"

"But you ruined my life!"

"How could I not have killed her?"

"Couldn't you at least have let her get old?"

"Get old?"

"Yes, get old."

"It wasn't possible."

"Why?"

"I don't know. Today I am a human being like you, and it probably wasn't possible, but today I can't explain it."

"Then when?"

"Later…"

"Didn't you feel sorry for her?"

"You know, today I feel sorry for all of your deaths. You are all so good; being a human is so good, but when I do my duty, then… what's the point of telling you that I enjoy it?"

"Where do you take us, then, my child, hmm?"

"I can't tell you that, mother."

"Do you have a mother, my child?"

"No."

"Are you an orphan?"

"Yes, I am an orphan."

"Why do you kill us, then, hmm?"

"Because I want to be kind to you."

"Is this kindness, my child?"

"But you can't be human beings forever, can you?"

"Why not…?"

"Won't you get bored?"

"When we get old, do whatever you want with us."

"If everyone got old, then life would have no value."

"That's cruel, my child."

"But that's the rule."

"What did you have against Christ, then?"

"I did that out of kindness. Without it you wouldn't see Him the way you had to. You think it's a great cruelty. You know what, mother? I don't really kill you; I die inside you. I myself suffer at your soul's departure. I carry out what has to happen anyway, and what has to happen always does… though necessity doesn't entirely preclude chance… while I'm alive, let's forget about death. You know what? If you want, I'll tell you a secret: today, I alone can be killed, and if you kill me, you will never die, but please don't do that. Without me, life will be difficult for you; there will be no love and no joy… time is passing. Let's dance, play the music!"

The girls played the accordion and then the dancing picked up so much that it was as if the earth itself were dancing.

By the hilltop shrine, a few men were whispering secretively to each other.

Death was dancing. From time to time, he glanced at the sun and his heart sank, since it didn't have far to go before it set. The monk didn't leave his sworn brother's side. Small children were running around him, chattering happily. Death was laughing heartily; his face was glowing with kindness.

Then everyone was dancing, big and small. For some reason, they felt such love for the guest that they were all watching the sun with regret.

Only a few men were whispering secretively. Among them was Jghunai. Then they too began to dance and slowly came closer to Death. Suddenly, Jghunai drew his dagger and plunged it into Death's heart as he danced with his arms outstretched, and immediately Death fell down on the spot.

HUMAN SADNESS

Suddenly the accordion fell silent and the people stopped dancing. The monk clung to Death, crying, and carefully pulled the dagger from his heart.

Jghunai ran away up to the hilltop shrine, towards Elijah's Mountain.

The people looked down silently at the dying man, who was smiling so kindly at them that they smiled too, despite themselves. Then he squeezed the hand of the tearful monk, shut his eyes and stopped breathing.

In that moment, every being there was seized by a deep regret. The small children were crying; the monk was crying. The black-clad old woman lamented loudly:

> *"What did you want with us, my child?*
> *We could not understand your worth.*
> *How lovely was your youth to me!*
> *How can you rest beneath the earth?*
> *And limb by limb you will turn black;*
> *The snakes will take your eyes away.*
> *No longer think about this life—*
> *Your worth they could not fathom, nay!*
> *For us, my child, grieve not, nor weep,*
> *But join my children in their sleep."*

The people became so sad that they couldn't stand to look at this scene any more. They hastily dug in the earth and laid Death down to rest in wildflowers, instead of wooden boards. Then they cast wildflowers over him, and for a long time no one dared to throw earth on top...

Little by little, the sun came to rest behind the mountains

and Gudamaqari Gorge was veiled in darkness. The next morning, I myself witnessed how the sun rose, not from where it usually came up, but from the grave that had been dug the day before; it went up and up and at midday it sat in the sky.

MORE FROM THE AUTHOR

I saw a scrap of paper in the notebook of the philosophy of the Gudamaqari warriors. Just two questions and two answers were written on it. No first name, no last name, no place name where this has been written. I couldn't put it in the middle so I kept it for the end.

"What is life?"

"Life is sorrow, the sweet sorrow of human being."

"And death?"

"Death is also sorrow, the sorrow of human non-being."